Also by Debbie Macomber and available from Center Point Large Print:

Twenty Wishes
Summer on Blossom Street
Bride on the Loose
Same Time, Next Year
Mail-Order Bride
Return to Promise
Hannah's List
A Turn in the Road
A Girl Like Janet

Undercover Dreamer

Center Point Large Print

Undercover Dreamer

Debbie Macomber

CENTER POINT LARGE PRINT
THORNDIKE, MAINE

This Center Point Large Print edition
is published in the year 2012 by arrangement with
Debbie Macomber, Inc.

The text of this Large Print edition is unabridged.
In other aspects, this book may vary
from the original edition.
Printed in the United States of America
on permanent paper.
Set in 16-point Times New Roman type.

ISBN: 978-1-61173-460-7

Library of Congress Cataloging-in-Publication Data

Macomber, Debbie.
 Undercover dreamer : a vintage Debbie Macomber novel / Debbie
Macomber. — Large print ed.
 p. cm. — (Center Point large print edition)
 ISBN 978-1-61173-460-7 (lib. bdg. : alk. paper)
 1. Large type books. I. Title.
 PS3563.A2364U54 2012
 813´.54—dc23
                                                        2012005021

Summer 2012

Dear Friends,

I wrote *Undercover Dreamer* with a rented typewriter back in the early 1980's. It's hard to believe how much technology has changed since then isn't it? Those were the days before we had cell phones, personal PC's and the Internet. Oh my, how times have changed.

Still no matter what era in which a book is written, a good story remains a good story. I believe you'll enjoy *Undercover Dreamer* despite the fact no one has a cell phone or a computer. It's VINTAGE Debbie Macomber, written on a typewriter from the kitchen table. It's a little like looking into a time capsule.

These days I am connected to just about every bit of social media available. You can reach me at my website www.DebbieMacomber.com or on Facebook. You can even download a Debbie Macomber app for your cell phone. Are you impressed? And, as always, you can reach me via snail mail at P.O. Box 1458, Port Orchard, WA 98366. Choose any option . . . I do so enjoy hearing from my readers.

So sit back, put up your feet, and enjoy.

Warmest regards,
Debbie Macomber

For
Sharon Frelinger,
Christian sister,
beloved friend

Chapter One

R ivulets of rain slowly ran down the tumbled mass of auburn curls. Meggie weaved long fingers through the hair, tugging the wild array from the delicate line of her cheek.

Rain. It had done nothing but rain from the day she moved to Portland. Didn't the sun ever shine in Oregon?

Inserting the key into the lock, Meggie let herself into the apartment. The room, cast in shadows, was gloomy, the open door dispersing light into the dim interior. It still looked strange to her, even with the bits and pieces of her life scattered around saying that Mary-Margaret O'Halloran lived here. It wasn't home, at least, not yet.

Inhaling deeply, she laid the mail on the kitchen countertop and put the kettle on to boil, before wrapping her damp hair in a towel. She'd do something with the tangles later. Burrowing her feet into soft slippers, she put on a warm sweater to chase away the chill that seemed to come from her bones. No one had told her Portland could be so cold.

Minutes later the doorbell chimed. A second's apprehension tripped her heart. No, she had to quit thinking like that or she'd soon be paranoid. It was crazy how quickly the caller was tainting her outlook on life.

After a quick look in the peephole, Meggie forced herself to smile and open the door. A tall man from the United Parcel Service with a thatch of brilliant red hair smiled back at her.

"I have a package for your neighbor, Quinn Donnelley. He isn't home; will you accept the parcel?" the man asked with an impatient air.

"Oh, sure," Meggie agreed, and was handed a clipboard.

"Sign in space twelve."

Meggie penned her name and was given the small box wrapped in brown paper.

"You wouldn't happen to know if this is the Quinn Donnelley who's the homicide inspector, would you? He was on television several times last summer. I think he was working on the Milton murder case."

"No, I don't know if that's him. I just moved in two weeks ago," she admitted and closed the door, locking it securely.

Her neighbor's name was Quinn Donnelley, Meggie thought as she examined the package. She had seen him, of course, almost every morning, in fact. He was an interesting man with an interesting face. Not handsome, his features were almost craggy. He had a wide forehead and a receding hairline where he parted the straight, brownish blond hair on the side. There was a rugged appeal to this man and the character that showed in his face was more attractive to Meggie than the prominent stereotypes who were often considered handsome.

The kettle whistled and Meggie poured herself a cup of coffee. A homicide inspector, she mused; he certainly didn't resemble what she thought an inspector would look like. He was a quiet man; kept mostly to himself. She saw him almost daily, but he never offered her more than a polite nod.

After drinking her coffee, Meggie wrote a note and attached it to his door and wondered how long it would be before she met her intriguing neighbor.

The phone rang at exactly eight o'clock, the same time it had rung for the past ten nights. The minute it sounded, Meggie tensed. She let it ring five times, her heart pounding louder and stronger with every ring. Her hands were clammy and trembling when she finally lifted the receiver.

"Hello," she whispered, shocked at how weak and wavering her voice sounded.

A crude list of obscenities greeted her in a muffled voice. It had always been the same, night after night, the identical words. Her hand tightened around the phone until her knuckles were white.

"Please stop phoning me," she pleaded in a shaky voice. "You're a sick man. You need help." Meggie didn't know what she expected but certainly not the demented laugh that followed. As if the phone was suddenly burning her hand, she dropped it into its cradle.

Why was this happening to her? Why would

God allow someone to frighten her like this? Especially now, on top of everything else.

By ten Meggie was tired. A light film of perspiration wetted her brow and she wondered if she was running a fever. Her throat ached and it hurt to swallow. How much longer should she stay awake and wait for her neighbor's knock, she asked herself, glancing at the kitchen clock. Maybe he'd come home and hadn't seen her note. Maybe he had, and decided to pick up the package another day. Meggie was heading for the bedroom when the doorbell chimed.

"Who is it?" she called, before unlocking the door. She realized it was fairly safe to assume that an obscene caller would probably do nothing more than phone, but it didn't hurt to be sure.

"Quinn Donnelley."

Meggie couldn't help but notice how pleasant his voice sounded, husky and deep, creating a cadence with the rhythmic flow of the sound of his name. Somehow she had expected his voice to be like that. She unlatched the door and let him in.

"Hi," she greeted with a warm smile. He looked older than what she'd expected, in his mid-thirties. His dark eyes were tired and he slouched forward slightly as if exhausted.

Although Meggie felt a bit like the woman with the medical complaint who invariably corners a doctor at a house party, she hoped to ask Quinn what she should do about the phone calls.

"You have my package?" His hand held the note she'd attached to his door.

"Oh, yes." She knew he'd be the no-nonsense type. He'd attend to business and be on his way. She'd only take a little of his time, she promised herself. "It's in the kitchen. I'll be right back."

She held the box. "If you have a minute, I'd like to ask you a question."

He paused and Meggie could see he was irritated. "Yes?"

"Are you a policeman?"

"Inspector," he corrected in unfriendly tones. "Listen, if you got a traffic ticket there isn't a thing I can do about it. I suggest you pay the fine."

Meggie bristled, straightening to the full extent of her five feet, eight inches. With heels she would be nearly as tall as he was. Pressing her lips tightly shut, she gave him an icy glare and handed him the parcel. She held the door open for him. "I believe you have what you came for," she said coolly.

The dark brows ascended and his mouth twisted wryly.

When the phone rang, Meggie started violently and whirled around. Only once had the caller phoned twice in one night. The second ring, and she pleaded silently for the phone to stop.

"Aren't you going to answer it?" Quinn asked, watching her closely.

She shook her head, her hands knotted into hard

13

fists at her side. "It's probably a wrong number." At least she prayed it was. There wasn't anyone she knew who would phone her this late.

Four rings and still Quinn stood poised in the doorway waiting for her to move. But Meggie stood mesmerized, watching the phone as if it could reach out and grab her, as if the phone itself was the villain, her eyes round and filled with fear.

"Is something the matter?" he asked after the phone had rung five times.

"No," Meggie denied. Her life was falling apart, but at the same time she had never been more whole than she was now.

Six rings and still Quinn remained.

"Would you answer it?" Meggie questioned nervously. The sound of each ring seemed to increase in volume until she was sure the next one would impair her hearing.

Something must have communicated her terror to him because he slowly walked across the room and lifted the receiver. He didn't say a word and a few seconds later, replaced the phone.

"Is this what you wanted to ask me about?" He motioned with his head toward the phone.

Meggie nodded. "I've been getting these calls almost from the day I had the phone installed."

"These things happen all the time. . . ."

"I'm sure they do," Meggie interrupted, resenting his attitude. People had been making obscene phone calls probably from the time the first telephones had come into use. But that didn't make it any less terrifying to her. It didn't reassure her to have him say it was a common occurrence.

She remained beside the open door. "I believe you have your package, Mr. Donnelley," she said crisply. If he could be brusque and impatient so could she.

His face remained expressionless and he shrugged lightly. As he walked out the door he gave her a half-smile. Even that had the power to disturb her, and she sighed as she closed the door after him.

She had trouble falling to sleep that night. She pounded her pillow and tossed several times trying to find a comfortable position. About midnight she took a couple of aspirin and drank a glass of milk. Her college roommate had once told her that if she had trouble sleeping she shouldn't count sheep, but talk to the Shepherd. Jacquie was responsible for bringing Meggie to the Lord, for clearing away the misconceptions she had regarding Christ and religion.

Meggie missed Jacquie terribly now. Her friend had married the summer before and was living back East. They wrote often, but it wasn't the same as having Jacquie there to talk over her problems. Although they were the same age, Jacquie had always seemed so much more mature. Meggie realized that was because Jacquie had been a committed Christian most of her life. Meggie had only been a Christian two years and sometimes she felt very much like a struggling toddler.

It had been Jacquie who recommended that Meggie leave Los Angeles. The situation with her father and Sam had grown more strained every day. Meggie loved her father deeply. They'd always been close. It had only been since she'd graduated from college and was living at home again that he began applying pressure for her to marry Sam.

It wasn't that Meggie didn't like Sam; she always had. Perhaps that was the problem. Sam hung around so much while she was growing up that she looked upon him as a brother more than a boyfriend. They'd dated in high school and she'd attended the junior-senior prom with him. Sam was the typical boy next door.

He had briefly mentioned marriage before she left for college, but Meggie had felt like she was standing on the brink of life and had no intentions of settling down.

In the four years she was away, Meggie changed. The biggest change in her life had been Christ and her commitment to Him. Sam hadn't understood this either. By the time she graduated and moved home, the rift between them was even larger.

Sam looked like a boy to Meggie, a charming, lovable boy. But she was almost twenty-three and ready for a man.

Things would have been less difficult if Roy O'Halloran could have understood Meggie's feelings. It was almost as if he expected her to marry Sam because he had decreed it so.

"Meggie, a father knows what's best for his daughter."

"But, Dad," she'd pleaded a hundred different times, "I don't love Sam, at least not the way a wife should."

"You will," he insisted, shaking his head. "Give yourself time."

The heart of the problem had been O'Halloran Printing. If Meggie married Sam, then the business Roy O'Halloran had spent his life building would stay in the family. Sam had been working for her father since his high school days. He'd been primed and tutored to take over the business as soon as Roy retired.

Her father's confused look still haunted her. "Meggie, darling, you know I'd never want you to do anything that would be wrong for you. But Sam loves you, he's loved you since he was a boy. All these years he's been waiting for you."

No matter how hard she tried, Meggie couldn't make her father or Sam understand. She loved them both and it hurt her to see the pain in their eyes. Perhaps if her mother was alive things would have been different. But Barbara O'Halloran had died when Meggie was thirteen. Meggie had always been close to her father, but after the tragedy they became even closer.

Meggie had never experienced such guilt as when her father looked across the dinner table with an expression of such intense disappointment that it made her heart ache.

If her father's look bothered her, it was nothing compared to the sad, puppy-dog expression Sam wore most of the time. He had lived more at her house than his own, but after a while he stopped coming around at all. When she did see him, there was an injured air about him. It was her father who repeatedly told Meggie about the hurt she was inflicting on Sam.

When her father realized she wasn't going to marry Sam, he had applied pressure in the form of guilt.

"I thank God your mother isn't alive to see what a disappointment you and your brother have been to me." He gazed at her with lost, unhappy eyes. "If she wasn't already dead it would kill her."

As crazy as it sounded now, Meggie had nearly succumbed. Her older brother, Martin, was a career Navy man. Martin had never shown any interest in the printing business, much to her father's chagrin. And now, because Meggie wasn't following the path he had set for her, she too had disillusioned him.

For eight of the longest months of her life, she had remained at home, praying she had made the right decision.

Perhaps if Sam had behaved differently, Meggie might have yielded. But he was content to let her father do his talking for him. Whenever they were together, he acted as if her rejection had ruined his life.

Meggie felt herself withdrawing from life, building a protective wall around herself. Only her job with an insurance agency kept her from having an ulcer. It was the office manager who told her about the job with Hadley Insurance Company in Portland, Oregon and urged her to apply. This and the fact Jacquie had been telling her to make a break had spurred her into action. In the beginning she didn't feel she had a chance of getting the job as an underwriter. Her degree was in history and she had only been working in the insurance field for eight months.

In the days following the interview, Meggie had prayed hard that if she got the job then it was God's will for her to leave her father, Sam and Los Angeles.

Once he learned that she had the job, her father had broken down and cried. Meggie could remember seeing her father cry only once—at her mother's funeral. Meggie had wept too, tears streaming down wan cheeks.

"I've driven my little girl away," her father had cried. "I'm so sorry, Meggie. Can you forgive an old man for wanting his own way?"

"Oh, Dad." The tight knot in her throat had prevented her from saying anything more.

"I'm sorry, Meggie, forgive me."

They had hugged one another fiercely, the air finally clear between them.

Meggie began packing the next morning. Now more than ever she felt sure she had made the right decision. Roy had put on a brave smile when it came time for her to leave.

"Keep in touch, won't you?" he murmured, giving her one last hug.

"You know I will," she answered.

Sam had come earlier in the day, helping her load her Mustang. "I'll never love anyone the way I love you," he said with the lost-little-boy look she'd come to recognize.

They sat on the front lawn drinking Cokes, just as they'd done in their teens.

"Don't you understand, even now, Sam?" she asked, unable to look into his eyes. "You deserve a better wife. Someone who will love you more than I can. I don't want to hurt you, I've never wanted to, but it just wouldn't work between us."

"Later?" he asked.

Meggie shrugged. "Maybe." But she didn't know how.

"Could I write to you?"

The offer surprised Meggie. "I'd like that, Sam."

His large, brown eyes appealed to her. "Then it isn't over between us?"

Meggie could only answer him honestly. "You'll

always be my friend, Sam, but I don't know if there ever could be anything but friendship between us. We both need time."

His hand reached for hers, squeezing it hard. "I want so much more, but beggars can't be choosers, can they?"

"Oh, Sam," she whispered miserably. "We'll write, and see how things develop. Take care of my dad and let me know how things are going with you. I want you to promise me one thing."

Sam looked up expectantly.

"I want you to start dating other girls."

Sadly, Sam nodded.

The picture of her father and Sam standing on the front lawn waving good-bye as she pulled out of the driveway would forever remain in her mind. It had been a difficult decision to leave. But it had been the right one.

Meggie glanced at the bedside clock. One-thirty. She gave a tiny groan of frustration and closed her eyes. She didn't know how long it was after that before she slept. Gradually the waves of fatigue lured her into the arms of rest.

Hadley Insurance Company had a unique way of training its employees—from the ground up. Meggie had started her job almost two weeks before, and thus far had spent several days in the mailroom learning the different functions there. Next, she was transferred to the filing department. Many of the company files were on computers

21

now, but the business maintained a backup system and kept meticulous records in standard files. From the filing room, Meggie had worked in the accounting department, learning the ins and outs of the company's finances. It didn't take her long to appreciate the finer art of keeping the accounts balanced. Currently she was working at the fire desk, learning the rating process for homeowners insurance. Having worked for the insurance agency, Meggie was familiar with computing rates for both fire and auto. But it was interesting to view the process from the company's method.

By late the next afternoon, Meggie felt her cold was probably taking a turn for the better. After showering, she dressed warmly. Although it was March she chose fashionable jeans and a cable-knit sweater over a long-sleeved blouse. At least it wasn't raining this afternoon. For a fleeting second on the way home she was sure she'd witnessed a speck of blue sky on the horizon. Even a hint of sun cheered her.

The doorbell chimed as she set the oven on broil. It had been tempting to shove a TV dinner in the oven; she wasn't in the mood to mess with a meal. As it was, a broiled cube steak held little appeal. If she didn't need to gain weight she probably would have skipped dinner altogether.

She was just about to ask who was at the door when a voice spoke.

"It's Quinn Donnelley."

Meggie arched the fine line of her brow curiously as she unlocked the door. "Hello."

His smile weakened her resolve to act remote. "Can I come in?"

"Sure." She stepped aside and he sauntered into the apartment. "Would you like a cup of coffee or something?" she asked, feeling a little awkward.

He shook his head. "Another time. I can only stay a minute. I wanted to give you this." He withdrew something from his pocket and handed it to Meggie.

It was a whistle. She glanced up at him, confusion in her eyes. "I always did want to learn how to play the whistle."

The tight grooves at the corners of his mouth cracked with the beginnings of a smile. Meggie had the feeling he didn't smile often.

"I'm not sure where you can take lessons, but I do know when you should practice."

"Oh?"

"Yes, on a certain pestering phone caller. Entertaining a caller by blowing a whistle into the phone should work wonders, if you know what I mean?"

"I believe I do." She tossed her head back, sending the long length of her hair cascading down her shoulders. She could feel him studying her and the look in his eyes made her knees want to buckle. Meggie liked this man, had been strongly attracted to him from almost the moment she had first seen him. There was something about him that said he was the type who could handle any situation calmly. Absently she wondered if he allowed anything to ruffle him. A strength and power seemed to emanate from him, and she found his rugged, almost unattractive features compelling. Suddenly aware that she was staring, Meggie looked away self-consciously.

"Is something burning?" he asked, sniffing.

"I don't think so, I just turned on the oven when the doorbell rang." She looked around and noticed a thin trail of smoke coming from the kitchen. "Fire!" she cried, her voice slightly squeaky from the effects of the cold.

Quinn responded before she could, racing into the kitchen. A billow of black, bulging smoke followed.

Meggie hurried in after him and as the smoke cleared she saw Quinn standing at the sink, running water over a large box of cornflakes.

"Terrific," she groaned at her stupidity, her voice shaking.

"Do you always broil your cornflakes?" Quinn asked with marked patience.

"Of course not," she snapped, waving her hands to help clear the smoke and offensive smell. "I'd forgotten it was in there. The box was too large to fit in the cupboard, so I stuck it in the oven."

"Even Girl Scouts know to check the oven before turning it on." His voice was thick with mocking humor. "I can see living next door to you is going to be an adventure."

As he finished speaking the smoke alarm started buzzing loudly and Meggie whirled around, confused. "Oh, great, now what?"

"Open the sliding glass door and let some fresh air inside. That should stop the alarm, otherwise someone's apt to phone the fire department."

With abrupt hurried movements, Meggie rushed to the closet and yanked her coat off the hanger.

Quinn glanced at her with a hint of exasperation. "What are you doing now?"

"I've got a rotten cold. I'm not about to risk catching a chill," she shouted above the smoke alarm.

Sliding the large glass door open, Meggie swung both arms in huge sweeping motions in an effort to force the smoke outside. The irritating buzzer stopped and Meggie exhaled with a cough. Wrapping the coat more securely around her, she traipsed back into the kitchen.

"Look at this mess," she groaned, angry with herself for being so stupid. The kitchen walls were coated with a thin layer of soot and her throat was aching again.

Quinn dumped what was left of the charred cereal in the garbage and when he turned back around, Meggie couldn't restrain a laugh.

"What's so funny?"

"You." Her fingers covered her mouth as if the

effort would disguise her amusement. "You look like Al Jolson."

"Want me to sing 'Swanee River'?" he asked with a mocking tilt to his head.

"You sing?"

"Like a frog."

There was nothing to laugh about but suddenly Meggie knew she was either going to laugh or cry. She chose the former until tears blurred her vision.

"I'm sorry," she said as she attempted to remove a black smudge from his cheek with the tips of her fingers. "You've been kind and I've . . ."

His eyes searched hers and the look that did funny things to her heart rate returned. He seemed to reach out to her, touching some soft place in her being that had never been exposed before. The masculine line of his mouth curved into a warm, sensuous smile. "Do you think you could manage to live through the rest of the night without burning down the building?"

"Oh, sure," she said lightly, unable to take her eyes from his face. "I sometimes go whole years without this much excitement."

"I'm glad to hear it," he chuckled on his way to the door. Pausing, he turned back around. "You have the whistle." All the humor was gone from his eyes.

"Got it." She slapped her pants pocket. "Quinn?"

"Yeah?" Again his eyes met hers.

"Thank you."

"Any time, kid."

"Meggie," she corrected softly. A child was the last thing she wanted him to consider her.

"All right, Meggie." He said it, testing the sound of her name on his lips. He nodded almost indiscernibly, as if he found it pleasing.

A wistful smile edged her mouth upwards as she watched him close the door. Unconsciously her teeth bit into her bottom lip. Things could become very interesting with her neighbor. Very interesting.

Meggie was a little disappointed that she didn't see Quinn again for several days. She'd hoped that he'd ask how her whistle lessons were going but it was almost as if he was avoiding her. After two nights of blowing the piercing sound into the phone the minute the obscenities started, she hadn't received another call. Meggie felt triumphant, free. She wanted to share it with Quinn. Normally they left for work at about the same time, but she hadn't caught a glimpse of him since the night of the fire in her kitchen, enforcing the sensation that he was eluding her.

Saturday morning the sun filtered through the window, spraying the apartment with a golden warmth. The forecast was for late-afternoon clouds and a possible rainstorm, but Meggie cast the thought aside. Standing on the lanai, overlooking the City of Roses, she inhaled deeply of the fresh, vibrant air. Her cold was nearly gone now. After several days of chewing vitamin C's like they were candy and catching up on her rest, she felt like a new person.

"Get going, lazybones," she said aloud. Dirty kitchen walls were beckoning and she'd dressed in faded jeans and a sweatshirt for the project.

She had just dipped the rag into the hot sudsy water when the doorbell rang. Panic filled her. Please, don't let it be Quinn, she prayed; she wanted to look ravishing when he saw her again. Not dressed in jeans.

It was Quinn.

"Meggie, can I ask a favor?" he asked with a half-amused expression reading her sweatshirt that said, GOD THE FATHER, written in lettering that resembled the movie—*The Godfather.*

"You need a favor?" Meggie repeated the question. Suddenly it didn't matter that he saw her at her worst; she could only look better from now on. "I'd do almost anything for a fire fighter," she teased. Quinn didn't smile.

"I've been called out on a case. My daughter's with me this weekend."

Meggie tried to hide the shock in her eyes. Daughter? This weekend? Quinn was married . . . divorced?

She attempted to cover her surprise with a question. "What can I do?"

"Jill's thirteen and old enough to take care of herself, but she gets bored. Could she come over here for a while? I shouldn't be more than a couple of hours, three at the most."

"That's fine, I'm not doing anything important."

"Thanks." He nodded curtly, but not before Meggie recognized the appreciation in his eyes.

A few minutes later her doorbell chimed again. When Meggie answered there was a tall, thin girl with an outbreak of acne on her face. She stood, defiantly staring back at Meggie. Straight blonde hair fell haphazardly down her shoulders. Her blue eyes coolly surveyed Meggie.

"I'm Jill," she introduced herself.

"Hi, Jill, come in." Meggie smiled warmly, hoping to dispel the chilly atmosphere.

She entered the apartment slowly, appraising Meggie and the apartment with unfriendly eyes.

"Are you making it with my dad?" she demanded.

Chapter Two

If Jill hoped to shock Meggie, it wasn't going to work. "Heavens, no!" Meggie said with an amused smile. "I don't even kiss until the third date."

Jill glanced up, her blue eyes wide with feigned shock. "Oh, swell." She flopped down on the couch. "Mind if I watch TV?"

"Go ahead, I'm washing walls. When I'm finished I need to do some shopping. You can come along if you like."

The girl shrugged indifferently. "Why not? There's nothing else to do."

As she worked, Meggie glanced into the living room several times. Quinn said his daughter was thirteen; she looked and behaved more like sixteen. She wore a snug-fitting T-shirt and tight jeans. Nothing seemed to interest the girl for long. Meggie heard the television remote switched several times. One channel would be on for ten minutes and then abruptly changed to another. Every time Meggie looked into the room, Jill was sitting on a different piece of furniture, watching a different show.

Meggie finished cleaning the walls and began feeling guilty for not being a better hostess.

"Are you hungry?" Meggie asked.

"Naw," Jill shouted back, her eyes not leaving

the figures moving on the television screen. "I never eat breakfast."

Meggie stopped herself just in time before commenting on how important breakfast is to a growing teenager. With Jill's attitude, advice would only harm any friendship that could develop between them.

"I'm going to fix myself an omelette so let me know if you want something."

She was whipping up the eggs when Jill entered the kitchen. One of the chairs was twisted around and she straddled it horse-style. Her arms crossed over the top of the seat, her chin resting on her forearm.

"What's that?" Her eyes were focused on the cheese and green onions on the counter top.

"Stuff for the omelette," Meggie replied, beginning to grate the cheese.

"Looks gross. I bet it tastes that way too."

Smiling softly to herself, Meggie continued to work. "Surprisingly it doesn't. My dad taught me how to cook lots of stuff with eggs. Every Saturday morning we emptied the refrigerator, putting leftovers in omelettes. You wouldn't believe some of the combinations we came up with."

"Didn't your mother mind the two of you in her kitchen?"

Meggie stopped and turned around. "My mother died when I was about your age."

A short silence followed. "My mother's dead."

"I'm sorry, Jill, I didn't know."

"My dad has never gotten over her death. I live with my grandmother now because of dad's job and all."

"That must make it hard for you?"

The small shoulders shrugged expressively. "Not really, my grandma's all right. She wants me to be a movie star like my mother."

"Your mother was a movie star?"

Jill appeared pleased at Meggie's interest. "Yeah, she made hundreds of movies. She was real famous."

Hundreds of movies, real famous? Things were beginning to ring untrue. "What was her name, maybe I've heard of her?"

A peculiar look flickered across Jill's expression. "I can't tell you that. My dad doesn't like me to let anyone know about my mother. I probably shouldn't have told you." She lifted her chin in a gesture of pride, as if the daughter of a famous actress should sit up properly.

"Don't worry," Meggie assured her with a smile. "I won't say a word."

Placing a pat of butter into the pan, Meggie waited until it had melted and was bubbling before pouring the whipped eggs inside.

Jill stood and was watching as Meggie added cheese, diced onion, chopped tomato and olives to the mixture before folding it with an expert hand.

The aroma of melting cheese and eggs filled the tiny kitchen.

"Sure you won't try some?" Meggie questioned again.

Jill hesitated, then nodded. "Maybe just a little."

Pleased, Meggie brought down an extra plate and evenly divided the meal. Of her own initiative, Jill placed forks and two short glasses on the table while Meggie got orange juice from the refrigerator. Jill had already taken her first bite when Meggie sat down. She paused, bowed her head and murmured her own silent grace. The prayer was one of gratitude for the meal she was about to eat, but there was also a short prayer for wisdom in being a friend to Jill.

When she glanced up, Jill had stopped eating and was staring at her. "What was that?"

"I was saying grace."

"Grace?" Jill laughed sarcastically. "Don't tell me you're a Jesus freak too?"

"I'm a Christian, if that's what you mean."

Jill raised both eyebrows mockingly. "Oh?"

Determined not to let this child goad her, Meggie ignored the comment and began eating. She glanced out the window and noted unhappily the change in the weather. Gray clouds were rolling in, darkening the sky.

"Darn, it looks like it's going to rain after all. I'd better hurry if I want to finish my errands before the downpour."

"Can I come with you?" Jill looked up expectantly.

Meggie was both pleased and surprised at the eagerness in the young girl's face. "Of course, but I'm going to have to take a shower before we go. I'm a mess."

"That's all right," Jill agreed. "I need to put on my makeup first anyhow."

Meggie stayed longer in the shower than usual. Some people would think it was ridiculous to pray with hot water pouring over her, but Meggie was concerned about handling Jill.

There was a hurt in that child's life that was impossible not to recognize. Just watching Jill brought an ache to Meggie's heart. Standing under the spray of the water, she called upon the promise of God's word, seeking wisdom.

Toweling herself dry, Meggie dressed in brown cords and a light pink pullover sweater. Seeing how long she'd left Jill alone, she hurried into the living room. One glance at the younger girl and Meggie had to restrain a shocked gasp.

Jill wore so much makeup that she looked like a gaudy vaudeville actress. A bright shade of blue eye shadow reached from the tips of her lashes to the arch of her brow. The blush on her cheeks resembled bold circles of a circus clown. Her lips were painted a brilliant shade of ruby red. The fragrance she was wearing was so overpowering it was difficult to breathe. Meggie speculated that she must have used half the bottle. She swallowed tightly. Should she say anything to Jill, she wondered. And if so, what could she say without offending her?

"I'm sorry I was so long," she murmured. "I still need to put on my face. Want to talk to me while I do?" The words were out even before Meggie was aware of what she was going to say.

Jill followed Meggie into the bathroom and sat on the toilet seat and watched as Meggie tugged a brush through the thick auburn curls, tying them away from her face with a maroon-colored ribbon.

"My hair gets in the way. That's why I tie it back, otherwise my bangs get eye shadow on them."

One corner of Jill's mouth lifted in a half-smile. "I know, mine's the same way."

First Meggie added a light layer of moisturizer to her face, gently rubbing it into the soft, pliant skin. She had to steady her hand as she applied the liner and eye shadow. Who would have believed a thirteen-year-old could make her so nervous? When her eyes were done to her satisfaction, she added blush, blending it into her skin in a circling outward motion.

"Why are you doing that?" Jill questioned, her round eyes keen with interest.

"This is the best way to keep the facial tissues in tone and prevent wrinkling. You don't need to worry about that."

"Not yet," Jill laughed, but she continued to study Meggie's every move.

Once Meggie caught a movement from the corner of her eye in the reflection of the mirror and noticed that Jill was imitating the movements with her hands, as if practicing.

Meggie finished by applying a soft cherry-cream color stick to her lips, then added a touch of cologne to her pulse points behind her ears and wrists.

"I'm done," she announced.

"That's all?" Jill looked amazed.

Meggie nodded.

"But you hardly put anything on," she challenged. "I can barely tell you're wearing makeup at all."

"That's the way it's supposed to be," Meggie explained. "Cosmetics are made to enhance a woman's face, not overshadow and dominate. If you look at the models' pictures in magazines you'll see what I mean. Here, I'll show you." Several publications were sitting on the end table beside the couch and Meggie grabbed one and brought it in to Jill. She handed her the latest issue of *Vogue*.

Jill flipped through the pages, stopping and examining the models and advertisement pictures.

"You're right," she acknowledged, barely above a whisper. "I'm wearing too much, aren't I?"

Meggie nodded, almost afraid that if she agreed it would trigger a negative response from Jill.

"Will you show me how?" Jill asked shyly.

Meggie couldn't have been more pleased. They removed all of the younger girl's makeup and started fresh. She had prayed, asked for God's wisdom. Why was she so surprised when He answered?

"Meggie, catch!"

Meggie straightened from behind the refrigerator door just in time to capture a flying orange. "Watch it, kid, or I'll toss you a ripe tomato."

Jill giggled, the sound of her laughter ringing through the small kitchen as she withdrew Meggie's groceries from the bags. "Where does this go?" She held up a roll of aluminum foil.

"Over there." Meggie pointed to the middle drawer and watched as Jill placed the roll inside.

"It's fun shopping with you."

"I enjoyed having you along. We'll do it again sometime."

The deep blue eyes sparkled and Meggie mused at how pretty Jill was when she smiled. "I'd like that. Dad hardly shops, all he eats is TV dinners. You wouldn't believe his freezer, it's jammed full of frozen boxes."

"Why don't you cook?" Meggie suggested, closing the refrigerator door and studying Jill.

The girl looked surprised. "I don't know how," she gestured helplessly. "Besides Hariette doesn't like me fiddling in her kitchen."

"Hariette?"

"My grandmother. She likes me to call her by her first name."

Beneath all Jill's outward indifference and sharp tongue, Meggie recognized herself. Her own mother had died when she was thirteen and Meggie was suddenly forced to take over a lot of the household responsibilities. She was just about to tell Jill about their common experiences when the doorbell rang.

Jill raced to the door. "I bet that's dad."

Quinn entered the apartment and Meggie quickly drowned the excitement she felt at seeing him again. Strong fingers of one hand absently stroked his chin, before he greeted his daughter. His thoughts appeared to be a hundred miles away. When he did focus his attention on Jill, his eyes sharpened in challenge.

"I thought I told you I didn't want you wearing makeup," he scolded angrily. "You're too young for that garbage."

The ready smile died on Jill's tender face. Slowly she lowered her eyes as if studying the pattern in the carpet. "Meggie taught me how to put it on," she murmured miserably.

The accusing eyes glared at Meggie from across the width of the room.

"I didn't mean to do anything against your wishes, Quinn." She could feel his anger, almost taste it; the tension twisted her stomach muscles.

"I was wearing cosmetics when I was thirteen; I didn't think it would do any harm."

The cold eyes narrowed. "That's just it. You didn't think." His glance fell again on his daughter, as he gripped her upper arm tightly. "You look just like your mother." It was more of an accusation than a compliment.

"I think you're overreacting," Meggie snapped. Was Quinn so insensitive that he couldn't see what his disapproval was doing to Jill? How could he possibly not detect the hurt in the young girl's eyes?

The look he shot Meggie silenced anything more she might have said.

"I'll thank you to mind your own business." Opening the door with an angry jerk, he pulled Jill along with him. "Leaving Jill with you was a mistake. One that won't be repeated."

For a long moment, Meggie stood stunned and disbelieving. How could she be so strongly attracted to a man who could be harsh and cruel to his own daughter? Didn't he know he was driving Jill further and further away? Meggie's heart ached for the little girl who desperately yearned for her father's approval.

Silently she put the rest of the groceries away, her thoughts preoccupied with her neighbors. When she'd finished, her gaze fell on the half-finished romance lying on the table beside the sofa. Meggie needed to engross herself in the plot and escape life's realities for a while. Leaning against the arm of the sofa she buried her bare feet under the sectional cushion. Just for an instant she wished her life could fall as easily into place as those in the book. She realized that God had a perfect plan for her life, as well as Quinn's and Jill's. If she didn't possess this confidence, their lives, their whole existence would be nothing more than a jumbled mess without rhyme or reason.

About five-thirty, Meggie began thinking about dinner and what she was going to cook, when Quinn knocked on her door.

He shifted his feet once as if he was uneasy. But the expression on his face was as determined as she'd ever seen. Silently Meggie chided herself for hoping he'd come to apologize. It didn't take long to see that wasn't the reason.

"Now what have I done?" she asked defensively.

Surprise sparked in the dark eyes. "Nothing. I wanted to say I was sorry for what happened," he said tightly. "You're right. Jill's thirteen and it's about time for her to want to experiment with makeup."

An apology! Meggie didn't need a degree in psychology to recognize that Quinn didn't make amends often. Just the way he was standing, the rigid set of his jaw and the eyes that just managed to avoid hers, told Meggie that this was out of character for this perplexing man.

"Don't worry about it, I understand." She was almost too surprised to speak. "My father felt the same way when I was Jill's age. If I'd waited for him to realize I was growing up I would have been a college graduate before he allowed me to date."

Quinn agreed with a rough jerk of his head. "Jill and I are going out to dinner later. We'd both like it if you would join us."

Again Meggie was surprised. "I'd like that. When should I be ready?"

"Does an hour give you enough time?" Thick brows rose in question.

"That'll be fine." Excitement raced through her blood. The way her heart was pounding, one would think she had just been invited on her first date.

After a careful survey of her closet, Meggie chose one of her prettiest dresses. The design was simple, with a scooped neckline and full sleeves. The formfitting waist emphasized Meggie's natural feminine curves without calling attention to her nearly perfect body.

Jill appeared at the door about thirty minutes later. "Dad said you should show me how to put my makeup on again," she asked almost shyly.

A tiny smile quivered at the corners of Meggie's full mouth. She could almost visualize what had happened with Jill's heavy hand.

After a few simple words of instruction, Jill was

on her own, amazing Meggie at how quickly she learned. The younger girl was placing on the finishing touches when Meggie brought out a gold chain necklace. Her hair fell forward as she bent her head so the thickness wouldn't be caught in the clasp of the necklace.

"That's pretty." Jill admired the jewelry openly.

"It was a gift a long time ago from a boyfriend." Meggie didn't bother to explain that the boyfriend was Sam and all the complications that had arisen in her life because of this relationship.

"I've had a lot of boyfriends. I've even gone steady lots of times," Jill told her proudly.

"Steady?" Meggie questioned uncertainly.

"Oh, sure. I've been going steady with boys for years. Hariette says I'm a lot like my mother. She had lots of boyfriends early, too." Jill hesitated as Meggie sprayed a delicate rose-scented cologne on her. "Can I use that?" she questioned eagerly.

"Sure." She handed the bottle to Jill and was pleased to note that the girl used it sparingly, imitating Meggie.

"I have lots of pretty jewelry too," Jill continued lightly. "I have one necklace that's made entirely of rings I got from high school boys."

"Rings?" Meggie glanced up skeptically.

"I've gone steady with so many boys that I have a whole necklace of class rings. I mean it would be impossible to wear them all on my fingers."

There was a lot more than just a note of untruth

in the statement, but Meggie said nothing. Jill was hoping to impress her, to have Meggie believe that she was attractive to others. Her heart ached to tell Jill she didn't need to rely on fabrications to have people like her. But for now it was best to say nothing.

Quinn arrived a few minutes later. He'd changed and was wearing slacks with a plaid shirt that was open at the throat, exposing curly blond hairs.

"Are you girls ready?" he asked, his eyes smiling deeply into Meggie's.

"Ready," Jill answered for them both. "But, Dad, we're not girls, we're women."

"Of course, my mistake," he replied mockingly, his dark eyes dancing with repressed laughter. He helped Meggie on with her coat, holding the charcoal gray wool open for her so she could slip both arms in at once. It might have been her imagination, but she felt his hands had rested on her shoulder for just a fraction longer than necessary. Not that she minded. Somehow she needed to know this magnetic attraction was mutual. She wanted Quinn to feel something strong for her. She needed the lingering feel of his touch.

"Where are you taking us, Dad?" Jill asked as they came out of the front of the apartment building. Not giving him the opportunity to answer, Jill continued, "My dad knows all kinds of neat places. Mostly from people he's worked with or people he's gotten information from for one of his murder cases. Last summer Dad . . ."

"Jill," Quinn snapped, silencing her.

Meggie watched as Jill bit into her trembling bottom lip. Unable to restrain herself, Meggie reached for the girl's hand and gave it a reassuring squeeze. Jill yanked her fingers away.

"I thought we'd try a new Thai restaurant." His eyes sought Meggie's and then he grinned crookedly. "How does that sound?"

"Do I have to use chopsticks?" she asked jokingly.

"Dad can," Jill interrupted. "He can use them better than anyone . . ." With a riveting glance from her father, Jill abruptly stopped talking.

"I think they'll let us foreigners use the standard equipment, if we insist," Quinn said as they approached the parking lot.

Meggie had wondered what type of car Quinn drove. So much of a man's personality was revealed in the car he owned, at least that was what her father had always said. Meggie remembered when she was sixteen that her father hadn't allowed her to go on a date when the boy showed up in a flashy car with a souped-up engine. It had been humiliating to tell him that something unexpected had come up, and she couldn't go out after all.

An unintentional smile curved up her mouth as Quinn opened the doors of his four-wheel-drive Jeep. She would have guessed he'd drive something practical. Quinn Donnelley wasn't out to impress anyone.

After a quick drive on the freeway, Quinn parked directly in front of the restaurant. They were greeted by the hostess almost as soon as they entered the doors of the restaurant. The woman was petite, beautifully dressed in a traditional gown from Thailand. She was so strikingly beautiful Meggie had difficulty keeping her eyes off the light olive-colored skin, contrasted by the shimmering gold costume.

Quinn seemed to know her, and spoke to her in her own language. The woman smiled warmly, obviously pleased by his words, and led them to their table. Meggie couldn't help but notice it was the best table in the place and probably reserved only for honored guests. After they were seated and handed menus, the waiter appeared. A wide smile brightened his face. He too spoke to Quinn in his native tongue. Quinn responded, a rush of words flying over Meggie and Jill's heads.

"I think he just told him we want to use forks and spoons," Meggie whispered. For the first time since leaving the apartment building, Jill smiled.

"See what I mean," Jill whispered back. "My dad knows just about everything."

"I sincerely doubt that," Quinn inserted drily, lifting his menu. "I recommend the seafood. Ananda suggested the duck, but that may be a bit exotic for you girls."

Meggie winked at Jill. "I'm in the mood for exotic, how about you?"

Jill looked up, her eyes peering just above the menu. "I was thinking about ordering a hamburger."

"Hamburger?" Meggie pretended acute shock. "Where's your sense of adventure, girl?"

"Well . . ." She looked to her father, her eyes seeking his advice.

In that second, as brief as it was, Meggie saw such undisguised adoration it nearly knocked the oxygen from her lungs. Jill may have been just thirteen, but it wouldn't have mattered if she was twenty-three. This child desperately needed her father's approval.

"Don't look at me," Quinn told his daughter curtly. "The decision is yours. You can have anything you want."

Meggie clenched her hands in her lap, her long fingernails biting into the palms of her hands. Round eyes urgently pleaded with him to see what he was doing to Jill.

Jill's downcast eyes continued to study the menu. "I guess I'll try the Gulf of Siam seafood dish. That sounds exotic, doesn't it, Meggie?"

Meggie laughed aloud. "That's more than exotic, my dear. I'd term that brave."

Quinn gave the order and a few minutes later Ananda returned, laying out several small bowls of sauces, some hot and spicy, others less so. In painstaking English he explained each sauce.

The duck smelled of curry and ginger and was layered on a bed of stir-fried vegetables. Jill's dinner was a combination of several varieties of seafood with vegetables and rice.

"Meggie likes to pray before she eats," Jill announced after the waiter had departed. An uncomfortable silence followed as Quinn stopped to study Meggie. A disconcerting, wary light crept into his brown eyes.

Meggie hadn't intended to make an issue of prayer; she would gladly have followed their lead but Jill had brought up the subject.

"Why do you pray before eating?" Jill questioned after a while. It was asked with genuine curiosity, without censure or ridicule.

"It's a way of saying thank you to God for supplying my needs," Meggie explained.

"Your needs?" The soft inflection in her voice made the statement a question.

"My dinner, and my friends." She faltered slightly over the word "friends." Meggie suddenly felt as if Quinn and Jill had pinned her to a specimen plate, and were examining her and her beliefs under a microscope. Meggie wasn't accustomed to defending herself and stiffened.

Quinn shrugged. "A little religion never hurt anyone. It wouldn't do you any harm to start attending Sunday school, Jill."

The young girl bristled defiantly. "You aren't getting me into one of those crazy places."

Meggie couldn't restrain the soft laughter. "Honestly, you two make faith sound like some kind of disease. And Jill, you're acting like church is worse than going to the dentist."

"I'd rather visit the dentist," Jill shot back aggressively. "Have you ever seen the kind of people who attend church?"

Meggie burst out laughing. "All the time! You know if you two would put aside your prejudices long enough you might discover that Christians are plain, ordinary, everyday people."

"You mean besides being pious, judgmental and all-around 'dudley-do-rights'?" Quinn teased, but there was an underlying tone of seriousness.

Supporting her elbows on the linen tablecloth, Meggie looked Quinn directly in the eyes. "Shall I tell you some of the gossip floating around about the Portland Police Department?"

"Touché, O'Halloran, touché."

After dinner Quinn and Jill persuaded Meggie to try her hand at bowling. It had been years since Meggie had lifted a bowling ball. As she suspected, Quinn was an excellent bowler and Meggie wondered fleetingly if there was anything this man couldn't do. Jill and Meggie played so terribly that more balls landed in the gutter than hit the pins. Finally the two women decided the only way they could compete against Quinn was to combine their scores. Still, he won the match.

An hour later Meggie and Quinn sat in her kitchen

while Jill watched her favorite television show. Meggie unplugged the perking coffee pot as Quinn studied her agile movements around the kitchen.

"Jill likes you," he commented easily, his voice slightly husky.

Meggie set two mugs down on the counter top. "I like her, too. She's a beautiful girl." Immediately Meggie knew she'd said the wrong thing. Quinn's mouth twisted and a tight mask descended over his face.

His look went right past Meggie, centered on the bright yellow wall behind her. "Jill's mother was very beautiful."

"She must have been," Meggie whispered, watching the younger girl from her position in the kitchen. Jill was a beautiful child. Long, naturally blonde hair, a face that was almost angelic and big, blue eyes that were sure to tempt any man's heart. Except perhaps the one that mattered to her most—her father's.

Quinn's hands hugged the cup after she placed the steaming mug on the table, his look absent. "Jill needs a friend."

"So do I," Meggie admitted. "It doesn't seem that long ago that I was suddenly facing life without my mother, learning to deal with my own grief and searching to find the 'real' me—all within the space of a few months."

"You turned out all right." A peculiar look flashed across his face.

Meggie laughed, amused. "Thanks, I'll let my dad know you think so."

Lying in bed, unable to sleep later, Meggie mused over the evening with Quinn and Jill. There was a void, a hurt in each of their lives. Perhaps God had sent her to Portland to help this small family, to show them His love. It was a task that boggled the mind. Meggie lay awake, staring at the ceiling, praying for this man who attracted her and his daughter who reminded her so much of herself.

The telephone startled her. Quickly she glanced at the clock. It was almost midnight. Tossing back the covers, Meggie reached for her robe at the foot of the bed, her heart hammering in her ears. Slowly she walked into the living room.

Three rings.

Please God, she prayed, don't let it be him. Not again. The whistle remained by the telephone and she picked it up at the same time as she did the receiver.

"Hello," she whispered, her voice trembling.

A piercing shrill burst from the other end of the line. The noise jolted her and she dropped the phone.

Even with her hand placed protectively over her ear, she could hear the muffled voice coming out of the receiver lying on the carpet.

"Don't blow a whistle in my ear again, Meggie. You'll pay, you'll pay."

Chapter Three

More frightened than Meggie had ever been before, she flew out the apartment door and pounded urgently on Quinn's. A minute later the door jerked open. The irritation quickly faded from his face after one look at Meggie.

"What happened?"

She was trembling so hard she could barely speak. "He called. . . ."

Quinn stepped into the brightly lit hallway, still dressed in slacks and shirt. He glanced up and down the empty corridor. Noticing that her door was open, he closed his own and escorted her back to her apartment.

"Did you blow the whistle?" he questioned softly.

"Quinn," she spoke haltingly, "he knows my name . . . he said if I blew the whistle at him again, I'd pay. I think he's going to kill me."

Gently, he folded her in his arms. "I won't let him hurt you, Meggie." The words were so infinitely tender, so assuring. Meggie laid her head upon his chest, the even thud of his heart pounding in her ear, contrasting the staccato beat of her hammering heart.

"I'm so frightened . . . so afraid."

"I know." Weaving his fingers through her hair, Quinn pressed her closer into the protective circle of his arms. "Trust me, Meggie. I won't let anything happen to you."

Her smile was weak, shaky. She had run to him like someone seeking shelter from a turbulent storm. There was no one she trusted more, no one who could calm her fears, assure her. No one but Quinn.

"Meggie." Her name was issued on a soft sigh. His hand curved around her neck, long fingers curling into her hair, lifting her face. Their eyes met in the darkness and suddenly everything was still. No longer could Meggie hear the jack-hammering beat of her heart. Nothing mattered, save this one man. Breathlessly, she stared back at Quinn awaiting the gentle possession of his lips. She wasn't disappointed as his mouth settled firmly over hers, drawing from her a response so complete that Meggie was shocked.

When Quinn shifted his position to deepen the kiss, Meggie slipped her arms around his neck, her fingers investigating the rippling muscles of his back. She moaned softly as his mouth plundered hers.

"Meggie," he whispered, his voice shaking as he buried his face in the hollow of her throat. His arms tightened around her waist, holding her so close she could scarcely breathe. Gradually his arms relaxed and he lifted her face, tenderly brushing the hair from her forehead and cheeks. "Tell me what happened?"

Still caught in the rapture of his arms, Meggie looked deeply into his eyes. The dimly lit room slowly seemed to dissolve around them.

"Don't look at me like that," he demanded thickly.

Meggie was surprised at the emotion in his voice, but still she couldn't speak.

Gently Quinn's hands massaged the rounded curve of her shoulders. "What did he say?"

Emitting a protesting sob, Meggie shook her head. "No . . . it's terrible, the things he says to me."

"Meggie." Hard fingers tightened, biting into her flesh. "He knows your name?"

She pushed the wild array of hair from her face. "Yes . . . he said, 'Meggie'; he said my name."

Quinn released her, jerking his fingers through his hair, a dark frown furrowing his brow.

Shaking almost uncontrollably, Meggie sat in the cushioned chair while Quinn paced the floor in front of her.

"I want you to get your phone number changed first thing Monday morning. This time insist on an unlisted number. We'll go from there."

"But, Quinn . . ." The fingers of both hands covered her mouth as she stared up at him helplessly. Whoever was making these calls was after far more than a cheap thrill. The sick tone of his voice told Meggie that this was not a game.

Quinn's face darkened. "He isn't going to hurt you. I won't let him."

Meggie gave a brave smile that fooled no one. If this madman chose to come after her there was little Quinn could do to help her. There was little she could do to help herself. As far as she knew she didn't have an enemy in the world, so how would she recognize him? How would she possibly know who it could be?

Her thoughts must have communicated themselves to Quinn. He knelt in front of her, taking her fingers away from her mouth and holding them securely in his hands. "Trust me, Meggie." His eyes implored hers, holding her gaze.

When she nodded, he very gently lifted her hands to his lips and kissed her fingers.

The next morning Meggie sat in church, but the words of the pastor's sermon seemed to buzz around her and fly away. Again and again she tried to force herself to concentrate on the morning message, but it was no use. She had prayed so hard that she was doing the right thing by leaving California. Everything had fallen into place so naturally—the job, finding a furnished apartment close to the office and within her budget. Since the break with her father, their relationship had never been better. It was almost as if he was relieved she was gone. Just three weeks ago she hadn't known a soul in Portland. Only now was she beginning to form friendships: a couple of girls from the office, Quinn and Jill, the manager of the grocery store and the warm people from church.

Who would possibly want to frighten her like this? It simply didn't make sense. But Meggie recognized that she couldn't live with this fear, this tension hanging over her head night and day. As it was, she wasn't far from being paranoid, suspecting everyone she came in contact with. Strangers on the street, people she would have normally greeted with a cheerful smile, were now suspect. It was getting to the point of becoming utterly ridiculous.

Giving herself a mental shake, she forced herself to concentrate on the pastor's words.

"If you'll turn with me to the Book of Matthew," he was saying.

Meggie flipped the pages of her open Bible to the gospel. A portion of the verse that had been assigned seemed to leap from the page and hit her squarely. For a moment her eyes widened with wonder. The verse was a quote from the Old Testament: I WILL GIVE MY ANGELS CHARGE CONCERNING YOU. Everything seemed to fade around her as if she was floating on a safe, secure cloud, free of worry and fear. It was as if Christ Himself was speaking to her, telling her not to be afraid, that He had given His angels charge of her welfare.

A slow smile touched her soft mouth. She *was* safe, there was nothing to fear anymore. A peace, a tranquility beyond anything she had ever experienced stole over her. Meggie could almost visualize the presence of two strong men standing guard on either side of her. Unshed tears blurred her eyes and she slowly lifted her head toward the heavens and mouthed the words: thank you.

Soon the pastor and the congregation came back into focus and for the first time that morning, Meggie listened intently to all that was happening around her.

"Hi." Jill was in front of the building when Meggie approached. Church was only a few blocks away, and the weather was lovely so she'd decided to walk. Actually she had forced herself, imagining strangers lurking behind every bush, almost afraid to breathe too loudly for fear of what may be awaiting her. How different the return walk home had been.

"Isn't it a lovely morning." Meggie smiled at the younger girl.

"Dad's worried," Jill said with a pinched, painful look in her eyes. "I told him you'd probably just gone to church, but Dad never listens to me. Besides your car was still in the parking lot."

"Just where have you been?" Quinn demanded, his face blazing with anger as he pushed his way out the front doors of the building.

Meggie was too shocked at the stark anger in his voice to respond.

"Answer me!" His eyes narrowed as he studied her intently.

Pride shot her chin up. "I was attending Sunday services at church."

The angry, contorted features tightened all the more. Wordless, he pivoted away from her and stalked into the building.

"Oh dear, I've done it now," Meggie murmured, unconsciously biting into her bottom lip.

Jill's eyes avoided Meggie, continuing to stare down the street as if she was expecting someone. "I've never seen Dad like that. He kept pacing the floor, jerking his hands in and out of his pockets. He even made a couple of phone calls, but I didn't hear what he said."

Miserably, Meggie emitted a long, drawn-out sigh. There had been a time when she'd wondered if there was anything that could ruffle this man. Now that she was aware that she was capable of doing it, she discovered the fact didn't please her.

"I think I'd better go apologize."

Jill glared at her, unable to hide the hurt in her eyes. "I wouldn't if I were you. When he gets like this, it's best to leave him alone."

"Oh, darn," Meggie murmured, frustrated.

"Oh, darn!" Jill repeated mockingly. "Is that the best you can do?" Her voice was thick with sarcasm.

"Stop it, Jill, I don't need it from you too."

She laughed harshly. "Well listen, lady, I've

about had it with you goody-goody types. You've managed to mess up my whole weekend."

"Jill," Meggie gasped, glaring at the girl. For the first time she noticed the tears shimmering in the blue eyes. If Quinn was worried and angry about her, he'd probably taken out his frustration on his daughter.

Tentatively, Meggie reached out a hand, gently touching the young girl's arm. "Jill, I'm sorry, it was my fault. Will you forgive me?"

Roughly she jerked Meggie's hand away. "Just leave me alone," she spat, and ran down the street.

Meggie stood watching her for a long time, confused and unsure. Not long afterwards, an older-model car pulled to the curb. Jill waved to the older woman inside and ran to the vehicle. Together they sped away.

Meggie felt sick. She turned and slowly walked into the building. Instead of taking the elevator she climbed the four flights of stairs, welcoming the exertion.

She didn't stop at her apartment; instead, she walked down the hall to Quinn's

He answered her sharp raps with an angry scowl. "Yes?"

"Quinn, I'm sorry," she said softly. "You have every right to be angry. I didn't think, I should have left you a note or something saying I wasn't taking the car." Her eyes pleaded with his.

He shrugged carelessly. "Don't worry about it."

"But I am." His cool facade did little to disguise his anger. Silently she beseeched him to understand. All this was new to her. She hadn't even thought about letting him know she was going someplace.

"Is Jill gone?"

Meggie nodded.

Quinn looked away guiltily. "She phoned Hariette."

Miserably Meggie hung her head, but continued to watch him from beneath thick lashes that veiled dark eyes.

"Church," he murmured drily. "All the while you were in church and I was thinking . . ."

Meggie was grateful he didn't repeat what had passed through his mind.

Their eyes dueled across the short space of the open doorway. The look in his eyes seemed to pry into her soul. Gradually his look softened and he smiled.

"I'm relieved to know you're safe, Meggie," he said unevenly.

"I'm glad I'm safe too." Meggie realized that she should probably return to her apartment. Everything she'd wanted to say to Quinn had been said and his look didn't invite further conversation.

She shifted uneasily. "Well, I guess. I'd better go change clothes," she murmured, her eyes not leaving his tightly controlled expression.

"Yes, I suppose you should."

She took a step backwards. "I'm terribly sorry," she repeated the apology.

He nodded, unsmiling.

Halfway between their apartments, he called, "Meggie."

She blinked. "Yes."

He gestured irritably with his open palm. "I broke the lock on your apartment. I'll replace it this afternoon."

Astonished eyes flew to her apartment. She was silent for a moment, examining the damage. Her eyes widened at the sight; that Quinn must have been in a panic was evidenced by her door.

"On second thought, I'll replace the lock right now." He reached one hand inside the apartment, withdrawing a leather jacket, and locked his door. "You're coming with me." It was an order, sorely lacking the politeness of a request.

"That's unnecessary," she said calmly.

Quinn breathed in heavily, some of the first anger returning to the grim features. "It darn well is necessary."

Meggie hesitated for a moment, then said quietly, "I'll be perfectly safe until you return. Don't worry about me, Quinn."

The dark eyes flashed as his mouth twisted wryly. "Let's just say that after this morning I'd appreciate a little peace of mind where you're concerned."

A smile trembled at the edges of her mouth, but

she didn't think Quinn would appreciate her humor. "All right, but can I change out of my dress first?"

He studied her coolly, then shrugged his shoulder. "Go ahead." He walked with her to the apartment, entering the room first.

Meggie noticed the way his trained eyes quickly surveyed the living room and kitchen area, looking for anything out of order. He led the way to her bedroom, switching on the light and making the same sweeping glance.

"Go ahead and change. I'll wait outside."

Meggie barely concealed a smile. "I'm beginning to think this is a James Bond movie." Their eyes met, hers crinkling with silent laughter, his deadly sober.

"I've seen too much in my life not to take this seriously," he said with a stoic expression, then turned and left the room.

The peace that had surrounded her since she'd been to church was something Quinn wouldn't understand. To even attempt an explanation to someone who wasn't a believer would be impossible. If she were to say something to Quinn, he'd think she was no longer rational. As the designer jeans slid over her slim hips, she wondered how she could transmit this sense of tranquility to him.

His reaction to her being gone this morning had surprised Meggie. She had judged Quinn to be levelheaded, an even-tempered man. Usually her insights into another's personality weren't far off base, so his behavior this morning seemed strangely out of character. Fastening the last of the buttons of her shirt, she grabbed a light jacket in case there was a change in the weather.

Quinn was standing in the living room waiting for her, his hands thrust deep into his pants pockets.

"Have you been to the Grotto?" he questioned her unexpectedly.

"The Grotto? No, I don't even know what it is."

Thick brows came abruptly together in surprise. "Then I'll show you. Words would be inadequate in describing the place."

Silently they rode together. Quinn didn't say a word for the entire twenty-minute ride.

When they drove past the airport and into the lush green forests, Quinn maneuvered the Jeep into the parking lot. He paused, looking around as if seeing the magnificence for the first time.

"It's been years since I was last here," he murmured. "Every time I come, I'm amazed at the beauty."

Meggie examined the area around her uncertainly. "What is it?"

Quinn's gaze wandered over her. "Technically it's an outdoor cathedral. Not too far up the path is a replica of Michelangelo's famous *Pietà*. People from all over the world come to the Grotto.

Thousands have viewed the sanctuary in honor of the mother of Christ. There's world-famous artwork on display, but I've been inside only a couple of times. I prefer communicating with God through nature."

Meggie wanted to question him further, but he swung open the Jeep door and climbed out. Meggie followed.

His hand reached for hers, enveloping her smaller one as they walked along the tree-lined trails. "I know you're close to God, Meggie. I knew you'd understand my feelings for this place. I'm not the type of man to sit in a church. When I need to feel close to God, I come here."

"I used to feel that way," she replied softly. "There were times when I was troubled and I'd find an empty church and sit alone in the back pew. Other times I went on long walks by myself, hoping I'd find God. It took me a lot of years to realize God wasn't hiding from me, I didn't have to go searching for Him. All my life He's been right here waiting. Suddenly I realized that if I felt God was far away, I was the one who'd moved."

She could feel Quinn's gaze studying her for a long moment. Hand in hand they continued along the paved pathway. Lush green ferns and a wide variety of flowers and trees marked the way.

"I first came here back in the sixties right after I got my shipping orders for Southeast Asia. I was young and patriotic, and believed I probably wouldn't be coming back alive. At the time making peace with God seemed the sensible thing to do."

"Did you?"

He glanced up confused. "Did I what?"

"Make your peace?"

He shrugged, his eyes avoiding hers. "I suppose," he responded noncommittally.

The walk amidst the beauty of nature was as beautiful as it was serene. Meggie could understand Quinn's feelings for this place. Following the paths, Quinn led her toward the fourteen Stations of the Cross and later the huge statue of Christ standing atop a rock-hewn monument base.

Gazing up at one of the many statues, Meggie whispered, "I can understand why the Grotto is called a place of peace and solitude." She couldn't recall a time she'd felt more at peace with herself and God, walking the fifty-eight-acre complex with Quinn at her side.

"There's something else I want you to see," Quinn insisted later, tugging her hand as he led her to the ten-story elevator that transported them to the upper level of the Grotto.

A sense of awe filled Meggie as she faced the sweeping view of two of the most picturesque states in the Pacific Northwest.

"Who could ever doubt there's a God, gazing at

this," she said, contemplating the breathtaking beauty of the Columbia River Valley.

Quinn's hand cupped her shoulder, the other hand pointing into the distance. "That's Mount St. Helens," he told her.

The once-majestic mountain peak looked almost flat, presenting only a shell of its former magnificence. Meggie could see the mountain every day, but never so clearly. Although the purity of the white snow was clearly visible, so was the drab, depressing color of gray ash that covered everything in its path.

Meggie, like most everyone in the world, had heard of Washington State's volcano. But to actually view the lopsided effect of the entire north side of the mountain, blown away with a force five hundred times more powerful than the bomb dropped on Hiroshima, was more than could be described with words.

"May the eighteenth, 1980, became known as Ash Sunday, the day she first blew," Quinn explained. "Thirteen hundred feet of mountain exploded in searing gas, ash and rock at the rate of two hundred miles an hour. It was the first volcanic eruption in the lower forty-eight states in sixty-three years."

"Dear Lord." Meggie sighed disbelievingly.

"It's estimated that two million animals, birds and fish perished that Sunday, plus dozens of human lives."

"She looks so peaceful now."

"Isn't that just like a woman," he commented drily, "but believe me, beneath all that tranquility stirs molten rock bursting out bit by bit every day. Although we can't see the dome-building process from this side, we do see occasional blasts of steam and ash. But nothing in comparison to the 1980 eruptions."

"Did Portland get much of the ash?"

The look he gave her was incredulous. "It was unimaginable. Not only that first time, but a few days later and then again in June. It was everywhere—the car, the house, my hair. Most everyone was beginning to wonder if we'd ever live normal lives again."

They left soon afterwards, taking a leisurely trail back to the parking lot.

"I'm so glad you brought me here, Quinn. Thank you," she said, the sincerity of her words shining deep from within her brown eyes.

He opened the door of the Jeep for her, walked around and swung his long frame beside her. "I'm not sure why I did. Maybe because I knew you'd appreciate its beauty as much as I do." He paused, averting his eyes. "Maybe because I thought we both needed something to blot out the worries of last night and this morning."

Meggie hung her head. "I feel terrible about what happened this morning."

"Don't." Gently his hand covered hers on the

vinyl seat. "I overreacted. I don't do that often."

Her eyes searched the rugged, uneven line of his jaw. "But why . . . ?"

The returning smile was grim. "My emotions were involved." The minute the words were out, Meggie realized by the look in his eyes that he hadn't meant to say that. Quickly he jerked his head around.

"Jill likes you, which is something of a novelty in itself. The girl needs a stable influence in her life. I know she isn't getting it from her grandmother or me, Hariette being the lesser of two evils. I'd hate the thought of Jill losing the friendship of the only decent person she knows."

The silence stretched between them. She swallowed at the lump of pain building in her throat. Quinn's only concern for her had been in relation to his daughter's needs.

They were driving along Sandy Boulevard toward town before Quinn spoke again. "There are a few basic precautions you need to start taking. It probably wouldn't be a bad idea for you to get a roommate," he suggested.

"I don't want a roommate," she told him defiantly. "For the first time in my life I'm truly on my own and I'm not going to let some prankster frighten me."

"All right. But I think that until we find out exactly what we're up against, it wouldn't do any harm to move in with a friend. In all likelihood, it's some kid after a thrill, but it doesn't hurt to be on the safe side."

The brittle movement of her mouth was a poor replica of a smile. "You're not getting rid of me quite that easily. I'll have my phone changed to an unlisted number and if that doesn't stop the calls then I'll deal with it later. You may overreact, but let me assure you I do not," she said stiffly.

From the way the muscles flexed in the firm line of his jaw, Meggie knew she'd hit home. But there was little satisfaction in the jibe, only a throbbing ache in the area of her heart.

Quinn insisted on buying and installing a dead-bolt lock for her door. They hardly exchanged more than a few polite, stilted sentences the whole time he was working.

The afternoon together had been so wonderful as they roamed the grounds of the Grotto. Meggie hated this breach developing between them. Several times she tried making conversation but his abrupt, noncommittal responses drove his point home. He clearly didn't want to talk.

After he'd completed the project, he set his tools aside and stood, withdrawing a card from his shirt pocket. "Phone me if you have any more problems," he told her forcefully. "The first phone number is the apartment, the second, my office. Don't hesitate, Meggie, I mean that."

Nodding, she clenched the card tightly to her breast. "Thanks, Quinn, for everything." She sighed deeply. "It seems that I'm in your debt again. Either that or I'm apologizing." Wearily she lowered her eyelashes. "Don't worry about me, I'll be just fine."

"Just play it safe. Don't do anything stupid."

"I won't."

Very gently his hand cupped the underside of her face, the rough texture of his palm massaging the silky smoothness of her skin. "Call if you need me," he whispered and lowered his hand.

It took every dictate of her resolve not to hold his hand against her face, to let him walk away. So much had passed between them in the last twenty-four hours and most of the communication had never been spoken: The things he had shared with her today about the Grotto; his reasons for going there in the past were things he hadn't told anyone. Intuitively, Meggie knew this. It was as if he had exposed a deeply personal part of himself to her, but found her unworthy and had pulled away.

With a heavy heart she leaned against the door, turning the thick lock. Everything was still and Meggie waited for the sound of his moving outside the door. For a long time there was absolute quiet before she heard him leave. Quinn had stood, with just the wood door separating them, as if he too was musing over the same thoughts.

He was a private man, fiercely proud. He didn't need her; he'd made certain she understood that.

But Jill did. The daughter of this man, who was capable of drawing such deep emotion from her, needed Meggie. And for now that was enough.

About seven Meggie realized she was hungry. She hadn't eaten since a hurried breakfast of an egg and toast. There wasn't time for lunch and she'd simply forgotten later. The thought of fixing something just for herself hardly seemed worth the effort. Cooking had never bothered her before. While in school she'd eaten in the cafeteria and didn't need to worry about meals. At home her father had continually praised her culinary efforts and as often as not Sam joined them for the evening meal.

The freezer contained one last TV dinner. No, that could too easily become a habit. Unsure of exactly what she was hoping to find, she opened one of the cupboards and began shuffling boxes around. A movement captured Meggie's attention and she leaned closer to see.

At precisely that second a tiny mouse scurried across the width of the cupboard. Terror gripped her throat and she gave a frightened scream, but the cry caught in her throat and was more of a strangled sound. Backing away, her heart vibrated in her ears until she thought the pounding sound would burst her eardrums. She cried out again as the panic filled her lungs. She hardly recognized the piercing shrill as her own.

Someone was pounding on the door, frantically calling her name. Quinn.

She ran to the door, her fingers fumbling with the newly installed lock. Her breathing came in giant gasps as she finally threw open the door and fell into his arms.

"Meggie, what is it?" he demanded.

Her nerves were stretched to the breaking point. How could she possibly explain that a tiny mouse had absolutely terrified her?

"Meggie," he repeated, shaking her violently.

Tears broke over the dam of her thick lashes and flowed freely down her face. Suddenly it was all too much: the fights with her father, the move, the new job, the obscene phone calls, and now on top of everything else . . . a mouse. Nothing had ever frightened her more than mice. As a child her brother had tormented her with the creatures until the aversion had become a phobia. It wasn't until she was in a psychology class that she learned she wasn't alone. The medical term for the fear of mice was musophobia.

When still she didn't explain, Quinn caught her by the shoulders and shook her again.

Laughter bubbled to the surface while she was still struggling with the tears. She pointed to the kitchen. "I saw a mouse."

"A MOUSE!" Quinn repeated. "You were screaming like a banshee over a stupid mouse?"

"I'm sorry," she mumbled between the tears.

"Oh no, I'm doing it again. I always end up apologizing to you."

Running a hand over his pale face, Quinn walked to the opposite side of the room. Pausing, he glanced out the window, drawing in deep breaths before turning around and facing her.

"I've always considered myself a peaceful, quiet man," he said cryptically. "But I don't think my heart can take another week of living next door to you."

"Oh, Quinn, I feel terrible."

"Don't you dare apologize," he warned, the color beginning to seep into his stark white face.

"I won't."

He sighed, running his hand through his hair. "Do you want me to set up a mousetrap?"

"No!" she gasped. "There's only one thing worse than a live mouse."

"A dead one?"

Meggie nodded.

"O'Halloran, what are we going to do about you?"

"I bet several colorful suggestions come to mind."

A smile crinkled the crow's-feet about his eyes. "None of them pleasant."

"I didn't imagine they would be."

The phone rang, drawing her attention to the end table.

The laughter drained from his face as his look

72

narrowed and quickly transformed. "You want me to answer it?"

Clasping her hands tightly together in front of her, Meggie nodded weakly.

Calmly Quinn lifted the receiver. "Hello."

Silence.

Meggie watched another transformation take place in his eyes, one of deep anger.

"It's for you." He handed her the phone. "It's your fiancé."

Without another word he turned and stalked from the room.

Chapter Four

Meggie watched Quinn walk out the door with a sinking sensation. Her fingers trembled slightly as she placed the phone to her ear.

"I wish you hadn't done that, Sam," she said huskily.

"Done what?" came the deep voice, calm and innocent.

"Told my neighbor you were my fiancé," she flared, losing patience.

"But, Meggie," he continued in a hurt, dejected voice, "it's the way I've always thought of you. It's the only way I'm able to bear another separation. Someday you'll love me as much as I've always loved you."

Defeated, she slumped onto the couch, crossing her long legs under her. "I thought you promised me you'd start dating other girls." She couldn't believe he would spend good money on a long-distance call to go over the same pointless argument.

Sam's laugh was derisive. "I have, Meggie, but there's no one else who will ever . . ."

"Sam," she interrupted brusquely, "stop it, you're repeating everything that's been said a hundred times before. It simply isn't going to work."

The line was silent. "What do you want me to

do? How can I change so you'll love me?" he pleaded quietly.

The hurt in his voice tugged at her already hurting conscience and she released a long breath. "Sam, I don't know. Don't you think I wish I felt differently? I don't like hurting you. Disappointing dad is the last thing I've ever wanted to do. Give me time."

"I'm sorry, Meggie." His voice changed subtly. There was a note of resignation that made her feel all the more regretful. "I'm being a beast."

"No, you're not." She sighed again, suddenly missing her home and her father and even for a moment or two, Sam. "It is good to hear your voice. How's Dad?"

Sam's interest rose immediately and he spoke in detail about the printing business, and other shared interests.

After twenty minutes Meggie replaced the receiver, the weight of her guilt heavier than she had experienced since moving to Portland.

Leaning against the back of the couch, she closed her eyes. She prayed silently, asking to turn her problems with Sam and her father to the Lord, and as she continued with her petition a comforting peace seemed to come deep from within her heart. She asked God to send another woman into Sam's life; she prayed that Sam would relinquish his feelings for her. She appealed to her heavenly Father that He would

75

take away the pain of her rejection of Sam's love.

The longer Meggie prayed the more she realized she had done the right thing by severing the ties with home. Although the move had been painful on both sides, it had been for the best.

Meggie was disappointed not to see Quinn the next morning as she left for work. They usually met at the elevator in the morning. There was no sign of him. Meggie wanted to talk to him, to clear away the impression Sam had given him. It was important to her that Quinn should know she would never have kissed him, or responded to his kiss if she had been committed to Sam.

With so much on her mind, Meggie nearly forgot to contact the telephone company. She phoned on her lunch break and learned it would be a couple of days before she could have her telephone changed to an unlisted number. Dealing with the people at the phone company in the business office was all part of an extremely busy day.

By five-thirty Meggie's head was buzzing as she unlocked her apartment. It was her first full day in the underwriting department. Everything was still new; all she needed to know and remember seemed overpowering at the moment. But Meggie was confident that the information she was struggling with today would become second nature to her later.

As she inserted the key into the lock, she

glanced down the hallway, hoping for the chance to talk to Quinn. The corridor looked stark and lonely. Repressing a twinge of disappointment, she let herself into the apartment.

Smiling softly, she looked around the room. It was becoming more and more like home. This was the first time in her life she was completely on her own, had ever lived alone. Surprisingly she found she enjoyed being self-sufficient.

Flipping the dial on the television, Meggie went into the bedroom and changed clothes. The sounds of the reporter detailing the evening news drifted into the room as she slipped into her comfortable jeans.

It was too early to eat; besides, she wasn't hungry. As the world news continued, Meggie found herself drifting to sleep. At the sound of a lively commercial, she jerked herself awake.

"You need some exercise," she told herself aloud. "Falling asleep before six-thirty is ridiculous!"

Rummaging through her drawers, Meggie located an old sweatshirt and slipped it over her head. She tucked her keys in her pants pocket and enthusiastically bounded down the four flights of stairs. Her blood was already pumping as she hit the street.

Two blocks and it became difficult to take in deep breaths.

Three blocks and her legs began to feel like lead weights.

Four blocks and her lungs were heaving.

Five blocks and she turned around, and walked home.

Inhaling deeply to catch her breath, Meggie staggered into the elevator and pushed the button for her floor. Leaning against the back wall of the enclosed cubicle for support, she chastised herself for being so out of shape. Two years ago she would have run a mile without working up a decent sweat. Jacquie, her college roommate, had gotten her involved in an aerobic dance class at a local church two nights a week. Within a few months Meggie had been in terrific shape. Tonight she'd attempted to sprint five blocks and her whole body felt like a quivering mass of cooked noodles.

She stumbled out of the elevator and nearly bumped into Quinn.

"Oh, hi," she mumbled, still breathless. "I was hoping I'd see you."

His dark eyes were fixed on her as he held the elevator door open with one hand. "Is everything all right?"

Meggie put her hand over her heart to quiet the furious beat. "Wonderful," she lied with a smile. "Just trying my hand at jogging." She laughed wryly. "Actually it was my feet that were doing all the work."

"You weren't alone, I hope," he asked coolly.

She nodded, unconcerned. "Running isn't as

easy as it looks; if I'd gone another block farther I'd have been forced to take a taxi home."

Quinn didn't seem to find any humor in her attempt. "I'm not sure it's a good idea for you to be out on the streets alone at night."

"I'll be okay." She dismissed his concern with a shake of her head.

He nodded curtly, stepping into the elevator, his hand continuing to hold open the door. "Take the whistle with you," he said, releasing his hand.

Meggie stepped back, her eyes meeting his as the doors slowly closed. His look was disturbingly gentle.

Meggie was halfway to her apartment, her hand in her pocket to extract the key, when she realized she hadn't said one word to Quinn about Sam. Since she hadn't explained things, Quinn would assume it was the truth. Groaning, she ran a weak hand across her damp forehead.

After a leisurely shower, Meggie made herself a light dinner of soup and salad. The phone rang just as she was filling the sink with sudsy water. Immediately her adrenaline began flowing and she swallowed tightly before answering.

"Hello," she said hesitatingly.

"Miss O'Halloran?"

"Yes." She breathed easier.

"This is the apartment manager, Daniel Wagner. I understand you found a mouse in your apartment this weekend."

Meggie's eyes rounded with astonishment. "Yes, as a matter of fact, I did."

"Please don't be alarmed," the man said gently. "I've contacted an exterminating service and everything will be taken care of by Thursday."

Tucking a strand of auburn hair behind her ear, Meggie sat down. "How'd you know . . . ?" Had there been a complaint regarding her scream?

"Mr. Donnelley reported the incident."

"Oh." Again she was surprised.

"Be sure and let me know if you see another one after this Thursday."

"I will," she mumbled, "and thank you." After a moment she replaced the receiver.

Quinn. Would the man never stop amazing her? He was thoughtful, and warm. It would be so easy to let this attraction develop if only she could explain about Sam.

By Wednesday morning, Meggie recognized that Quinn was purposely avoiding her. The first weeks after she'd moved into the apartment they had met several times while coming and going. But other than the chance run-in the other day, she hadn't seen him at all.

Thursday night, Meggie returned from her nightly jog, extremely proud to have managed seven long blocks without a cardiac arrest. She bounded off the elevator feeling somewhat cocky. Impulsively she sauntered past her apartment and knocked boldly on Quinn's door. She'd clear away this misunderstanding before it developed further.

"Hi." She smiled cheerfully when he answered the door.

"Hello," he responded somewhat drily.

"Do you notice anything unusual about these hands?" She held them palms down for his inspection.

A puzzled look flickered across his face. "You mean other than the fact the nails need to be trimmed?"

"They don't," she denied, then flexed them, catlike. "All the better to scratch out your eyes, my dear."

"Exactly," Quinn said, completely serious. "Keep them that length."

The smile died on her face and when her brown eyes met his they were just as sober. "I want you to notice there is no engagement ring on either hand. I am not marrying Sam now or ever. I apologize that he gave you that impression the other day."

Quinn shrugged as if it was none of his concern, his face impassive. "There's no need to tell me that," he replied crisply. "You don't owe me any explanations."

Meggie looked away awkwardly. This wasn't going well at all. "I realize it wasn't necessary to explain about Sam. But I wanted you to know."

"Is that all?" he drawled, his voice thick with impatience.

Meggie nodded, averting her face so he wouldn't guess that his indifference was hurting her.

Quinn's smile was wry as she turned toward her apartment. "Meggie," he called her back.

She turned around, her eyes avoiding his probing gaze.

"Your phone number's been changed?"

She'd nearly forgotten; it was necessary to call her dad tonight and give him the new number, otherwise he'd worry. "Yes, would you like my new one?"

Quinn shrugged. "There isn't any reason for me to have it. If I want you, I'll knock," he stated matter-of-factly.

Meggie flushed slightly and regarded him with unhappy eyes before silently agreeing with a short shake of her head.

Quinn could be so difficult to understand. When he'd kissed her last weekend it had been one of the most beautiful, tender kisses of her life. She had felt her body, her spirit communicating with his. It was almost as if their inner beings had cried out to one another.

And now, just a few short days later, Quinn's attitude was returning to that of a polite neighbor. It didn't make sense.

Pausing, her hand on the apartment door,

Meggie glanced back to his apartment. She'd been to his place several times now; never had he invited her inside. It was as if he wanted to keep her out of his life.

She felt a crazy kind of hurt in her heart. She'd been rebuffed before.

Friday afternoon Jill was knocking at Meggie's door almost the minute she arrived home from work.

"Hi." She sauntered into the room, "I see the boogeyman didn't get you."

"No." Meggie placed the back of her hand to her forehead dramatically. "I'm safe for another week."

Jill giggled. "Dad's not home, mind if I use your phone?"

"Go ahead." Needlessly she pointed it out to Jill. While the girl was dialing Meggie walked into the kitchen, making an excuse of looking in the refrigerator because she didn't want Jill to think she was listening to her conversation.

Jill followed shortly thereafter. "Dad's going to be a few minutes late. He said it was all right if I stayed here, if you don't mind."

Meggie glanced up from behind the refrigerator door. "It's fine with me. Want a can of soda?"

Jill shrugged. "Soda rots your teeth."

"It also causes cancer in laboratory rats and gives you pimples. Want one anyway?"

Jill nodded eagerly and held up both hands. Meggie tossed her the aluminum can.

They sat together in the living room, feet propped against the coffee table, sipping their drinks.

"I have a key to Dad's apartment," Jill volunteered. "Fridays after school I take the bus here. That way Hariette doesn't have to worry about me coming home and all."

"What about your clothes?" Meggie questioned, crossing her legs at the knee.

"I keep some of my things at Dad's and if I want to bring something special I put it in my backpack." Jill toyed with a button on her shirt. "Usually Dad's home early on Friday nights; he tries to be, anyway. But he's working on some big case and is going to be late tonight. He'll probably have to work tomorrow too." She tilted her head back, not bothering to disguise the disappointment in her eyes. "It's my birthday tomorrow."

"Jill, that's great." Meggie straightened, setting her drink on the coffee table. "We should do something special. I've been wanting to visit Lloyd Center. Do you think your dad would mind if we went shopping?"

"Lloyd Center? Really?" Jill's round eyes lit up eagerly.

The huge shopping complex was unique. Built on two floors, it had a large ice skating rink situated in the middle of the bottom level.

Spectators could look down from the upper floor to see an array of skaters gliding their way across the ice. Mothers dropped their kids off for an afternoon of fun while they shopped.

"Dad wouldn't care," Jill continued.

"Good, I'll look forward to it."

The doorbell chimed and Meggie rose to her feet with a fluid grace that was as natural as water's gentle flow over a waterfall.

"It's Quinn," came the deep, baritone voice from the other side of the door. When Meggie opened the lock, he greeted her with a curt smile. "Meggie."

"Hello, Quinn." She smiled gently. He looked tired; and irrationally she longed to reach out, smooth the hair from his face and massage his temples. A mental picture of him lying on the couch, his head cradled on her lap, flashed across her mind. Quickly Meggie lowered her lashes, afraid he could read what was in her thoughts.

"Is Jill here?" he questioned abruptly.

Meggie stepped aside. "Come in, we're just finishing a can of soda."

He did so grudgingly, his mouth curved in a cynical line that Meggie hated.

"Hi, Dad," Jill called to him, her eyes twinkling. "Did you pick up something for dinner? I'm starved. And, Dad, can Meggie eat with us tonight? She's taking me shopping with her tomorrow, isn't that great?"

Again, Quinn's dark eyes rested on Meggie.

The slender shoulders gave a delicate shrug as she batted her eyelashes wickedly. "Yes, what's for dinner? I'm starved."

For a moment Meggie was sure she saw the corners of his mouth quiver with a suppressed smile. But if so, he quickly restrained the amusement.

"If you give me the money, I'll run down the street and bring back some chicken," Jill offered enthusiastically.

"And I'll make a fresh green salad and set the table," Meggie elaborated.

Quinn's gaze bounced from his daughter to Meggie. "Why do I have the feeling I'm being blatantly manipulated by you two?"

Jill stood, holding out the palm of her hand. "Because you are," she said frankly, and winked at Meggie.

There was silence for a moment as Quinn withdrew his wallet from his hip pocket and handed several bills to Jill. He didn't say a word as Jill grabbed the money and her jacket and flew out the door. He may not have said anything, but the slant of his mouth showed he was none too pleased.

"Be a sport," Meggie chided. "I've been wanting to talk to you all week and you've been a regular cold fish."

Thick brows shot up. "A cold fish?" he spat.

"What else would you call it?" she demanded with a smile. "I could almost feel the Arctic chill through the walls." Some of the teasing laughter left her glinting eyes. "If you're angry with me about something, Quinn, I wish you'd say so and be done with it instead of closing yourself off from me."

At first the steely gaze bore into her as if he was going to deny the accusation. But gradually a softening light entered the dark depths and he smiled, relenting. "I'll be back in a few minutes," he said. "I'm going to take a shower."

"Okay," Meggie agreed. Her heart felt like it was going to trip over itself from the effect of his smile. He hadn't said a word about Sam, the telephone call or their conversation earlier that week. Even without verbal communication Meggie knew everything was going to be fine between them.

Quinn returned first, his hair damp from the shower. He'd changed clothes and was dressed casually in dark slacks and a rust-colored sweater that was open at the throat exposing blond, curling hairs. For an insane instant Meggie was tempted to run her fingers over the short hairs and wind her arms around his neck.

Her fingers remained in front of her as she stood at the kitchen sink, tearing apart pieces of lettuce for the salad.

Quinn moved behind her, his hands sliding over

her shoulders and down her slender arms. Meggie closed her eyes, fighting the temptation to lean back against him and surrender to the bold tide of awareness he was capable of arousing within her.

Gently his lips spread sweet, tender kisses along the side of her neck. Meggie rotated her head, her long hair falling aside to grant him easier access. Shivers of delight ran up her spine.

When his hands applied a subtle pressure, turning her around, Meggie slid her arms around his neck, anticipating the union of their mouths. Her pulse was thundering in her ears as his lips fit firmly over hers. Her mouth parted slightly in welcome as she surrendered to the crescendoing beat of her heart.

Quinn kissed her again before shuddering and dragging his mouth from her. He inhaled sharply and buried his face in the slim column of her throat.

For a long while he did nothing but hold her as if he couldn't bear to let her out of his arms. When he spoke his voice was no more than a husky whisper.

"You smell good."

"So do you," she replied shakily.

His hands closed over her shoulders again, as he pushed himself away. "Thank you, Meggie," he murmured.

She was perplexed. "Thank me? For what?"

Tenderly he brushed a stray curl of thick hair

from her temple. "For bringing a bit of sunshine into Jill's and my life."

Her dark eyes widened. "Good heavens, you make me sound like the Good Ship Lollipop."

A strange, brooding look came over him. "In a way you are. You don't live in the real world. You have this rosy picture of life and God that is so completely removed from reality I find it shockingly refreshing."

The sensation of happiness and well-being plunged to the pit of her stomach.

"Quinn . . ." She wanted to explain her beliefs, but a long finger at her lips halted the words.

"I didn't mean to put you on the defensive; I wouldn't want to hurt your feelings. The minute we met, I knew that you were going to be bad news." The amused twist of his sensuous mouth took the sting of rejection from his words. "I could see the only sane thing to do was stay clear of you. But I can't. You creep into my mind at the oddest moments. I lie in bed at night with only a thin wall separating us and I'm tormented with what I'm sure must be the fragrance of your perfume." He paused, shrugging his shoulders expressively. "When you're around, Jill laughs. I can't remember the last time I heard the sound of her giggles. But that's not all. You make me want to laugh again, too." His fingers softly examined the contour of her chin and the delicate bone structure of her cheek before coming to rest on her lips. "Do you have any idea how beautiful you are?"

A willing captive to the magic of his spell, Meggie didn't hear the sound of the front door opening.

"I'm back," Jill announced as she came through the living room into the kitchen.

Immediately Quinn dropped his hands to his side.

"I'll finish setting the table," Meggie said quickly. Too quickly. Her hands groped inside the cupboards for the plates and glasses. When she turned around, her eyes met Quinn's and he winked boyishly, nearly causing Meggie to laugh out loud. It was almost like they were young teenagers enjoying a tryst, disguising their affection from their parents.

"What do you think?" Jill stepped out from behind the dressing-room curtain.

"Oh, Jill," Meggie murmured and breathed in deeply, inspecting the lovely blossom-print dress. "Put on the jacket."

Long, slender arms slipped inside the matching jacket. Expectantly, Jill raised her eyes to Meggie. "Well?"

Meggie shook her head in wonder at the transformation a simple dress could make in the lanky girl. "It's just perfect," she whispered, "just perfect."

Jill's girlish face brightened with pleasure. "Do you think so? Really?"

Meggie laughed softly. "If you don't believe me, just look in the mirror." With a guiding hand at her shoulder, she led Jill to one of the store mirrors.

As if surprised at the reflection, Jill stood, examining herself for a long moment. The gentle smile gradually died. "My legs are too skinny to wear dresses," she insisted.

"They'll fill out soon enough," Meggie replied in a soothing voice.

Roughly Jill jerked her finger through the length of her blonde hair. "My hair is awful. Why can't it look like yours?"

By no means was Jill's outburst a compliment, but Meggie chose to look upon it as one. "If you want your hair to be styled like mine then you'll need a perm."

"Oh sure, and Dad's going to fork out fifty bucks on my hair?" she murmured sarcastically.

"I certainly didn't. There are such things as home perms, you know."

Jill looked away skeptically. "And mine's supposed to turn out like yours? Ha!"

"I don't see why not. I did mine, I can do yours."

"You did? Really? You'd do mine too?"

"Of course." Meggie laughed. "Now go change back into your jeans while I tell the salesclerk we want the dress."

Jill looked up, shocked. "I don't think I want to

waste my money on a silly dress. Blue isn't my color. Hariette says I shouldn't wear anything that has blue in it. Besides, the waist is too big. Look." She sucked in her stomach and made a show of placing her hand inside the belt.

Shaking her head mockingly, Meggie dismissed the idea. "The dress is perfect and you know it. Besides I'm paying for it. Just think of it as my birthday gift to you. That and the perm."

Jill gasped, her eyes growing more and more round. "Meggie, no. You don't need to do that! It's too expensive."

Meggie looked down upon the younger girl and the silent pleading in her eyes. How easy it was to recall all the times she had wished for a mother to go shopping with her, especially in her early teens. Jill must be feeling some of the same loneliness and it pleased Meggie to play even a small part in easing this child's hurt.

Impulsively Meggie gave her a tiny hug. "Happy birthday, Jill," she whispered softly.

While Meggie paid for the dress she saw Jill wander outside the store, pausing at the balcony to look at the skating figures below.

Meggie joined her a few minutes later, surprised to note the tears glistening in the younger girl's eyes. Meggie didn't say anything for fear of embarrassing Jill; she didn't want to do that. The emotion reinforced the sensation that Jill simply needed someone to love her for who she was.

"Have you ever ice skated?" Meggie asked after a while.

"Lots," Jill returned flippantly. "I'm pretty good."

Gazing upon the figures below brought back a myriad of memories. "I haven't had on a pair of skates in years," Meggie spoke wistfully. "Shall we?"

"Shall we what?" Jill still didn't look at Meggie, continuing to focus her attention on the ice rink.

"Go skating, silly." Meggie laughed.

The big, blue eyes rounded incredulously. "You mean now?"

"Of course I mean now. Come on, we have plenty of time." She didn't wait for Jill; instead, she walked purposefully to the escalator and rode to the bottom level of the center.

Jill caught up with her breathlessly as Meggie stood in front of the ticket counter. "But Dad said he'd be waiting for us by the . . ."

"Don't worry, he'll find us," Meggie interrupted calmly, handing Jill her ticket. "He's not an inspector for nothing."

Still Jill balked. "But I don't want to. Not now," she said forcefully.

Tucking her arm around her elbow, Meggie pulled her along. "Come on, Jill, it'll be great fun."

It soon became obvious that Jill's ice skating ability was another of her fabrications. One look at her feeble attempts to move around on the ice told Meggie Jill had probably never skated in her life. After one abortive attempt, she clung to the rail in a death grip while her feet slipped and jerked out from under her.

"Here, give me your hand," Meggie instructed, holding out her arm.

"Not on your life," Jill spat back angrily. "I thought you said this was fun. I hate it. You didn't tell me you were another Rosalynn Sumners. You're nothing but a big show-off."

Meggie wasn't about to let Jill's anger affect her. "All right, if you want to spend the entire day at the rail, don't let me stop you," she said and glided away.

After a couple of times around the rink, Meggie skated to Jill again. "Come on, you're going to have to trust me sooner or later. Otherwise you won't learn a thing."

"But I'll fall," Jill burst out.

"Yes, and I'll probably go down with you," Meggie said matter-of-factly, as she held out her arm. "But falling down and picking yourself back up is all part of the learning process."

Jill bit into her bottom lip indecisively before tentatively extending one hand to Meggie. "Oh all right," she conceded ungraciously.

They both fell twice the first time around; for a moment Meggie thought Jill might quit but she picked herself up again and laughed. For a while Meggie felt she was losing the feeling in her arm,

Jill was clinging to it so tightly. But little by little the hold loosened as the girl gained confidence. Within a half-hour she was skating on her own. She was ungainly, took abrupt steps, but she was skating in the standing position and all on her own power.

"Glide, Jill, glide," Meggie called as she skated past her doing a skillful about-face so that she was skating backwards directly in front of Jill.

"Dad's here," Jill said excitedly.

Meggie quickly surveyed the row of spectators standing outside the rink. "I don't see him."

"He's buying a ticket, I think," Jill spoke, her hands outstretched at her side as she concentrated, sliding one foot in front of the other. "Imagine my dad on skates."

Glancing around, Meggie caught sight of Quinn sitting on one of the benches lacing up the skates. Her heart was pumping eagerly as she remained in front of Jill until he joined them.

Jill looked up, her eyes dancing. "Dad, look at me!" Proudly she surged forward ungracefully displaying her limited ability.

Quinn watched his daughter until he lost his balance and groped for Meggie, who thrust out her arms to stabilize him.

"First time on skates?" she quizzed, laughing.

His mouth twisted wryly. "No, last. There are three things I regret in my life and this is one of them."

Hiding her smile, she placed an arm around his middle as she'd done with Jill.

His hand curled around her back, resting against her waist. He smiled faintly. "I don't know, skating does seem to have a few redeeming qualities." His twinkling eyes met hers. "It's a nice way of having you in my arms without either of us being self-conscious around Jill."

Meggie laughed, enjoying the feel of his warmth pressing against her. There was a rightness at being at his side even if it was only under the guise of skating.

"Dad, watch," Jill shouted as she flew past.

How eager she was to impress her father. When Quinn said nothing, Meggie cried out encouragingly, "You're doing great."

Quinn's look was thoughtful as he viewed his daughter's antics. "She's almost a different girl around you," he said to Meggie, his eyes searching hers. Relaxing his grip around her waist, his hand reached for hers.

"You should be proud of her, Quinn, Jill's a wonderful girl. I enjoy . . ."

At just that second, Quinn lost his footing. Flinging his arms out wildly, he struggled to maintain his balance. Meggie attempted to help him, but in the process hampered him more than she helped. Finally his feet went out from under him and he crashed onto the ice.

Meggie didn't bother to restrain her amusement,

as she peered down at him, hands on her knees. "You think it's funny, do you?" he asked with a wicked gleam in his eyes. He extended a hand so she could help him up, but when Meggie fit her hand in his, he gave a quick jerk, yanking her onto the ice with him.

"You devil!" she cried. In spite of herself, Meggie laughed at the dark eyes so full of mischief.

His gaze narrowed on her lips and for a moment Meggie was sure he meant to kiss her.

Jill interrupted them, flinging her arms out helplessly in an effort to stop beside them. Hands on hips, she gazed down indignantly. "Can't you two manage to stay on your feet for heaven's sake?" she teased, and with a toss of her long hair she glided away.

Meggie watched her go with a feeling akin to pride. Jill was changing. The angry facade was breaking away piece by piece, bit by bit.

"She's quite a girl, Quinn," she said as she rose, brushing the ice from her pants. "I hope this birthday will always be special to her."

"Birthday?" he quizzed with surprise. "It isn't Jill's birthday until September."

Chapter Five

Q uinn, this isn't necessary," Meggie said miserably.

The angry eyes clashed with hers. "Yes it is. Say it, Jill," he demanded, his fingers applying a punishing pressure to the girl's collarbone.

Jill stiffened defiantly, her back ramrod straight. "I'm sorry, Meggie," she gritted between clenched teeth. "But I'm sure there was some mistake. I never said it was my birthday."

Meggie swallowed a gasp. There had been no misunderstanding.

Again Quinn's grip bit into Jill's shoulder. "Give her the money," he ordered.

Bitter resentment flashed from the depths of her blue eyes as Jill handed Meggie several wadded bills. "This is the money for the dress. But I'll never wear it, I hate it almost as much as I hate . . ." She cried out painfully as Quinn's fingers viciously dug into her flesh.

"Get out," he spat, and pushed her toward the door.

Eyes wide with horror, Meggie looked on helplessly as Jill ran from the room, tears streaming down her pale face. The door slammed behind her.

"Will she be all right?" Meggie asked, her voice barely above a whisper.

Quinn ran a weary hand over his eyes and mouth, then nodded. "She'll go sulk for a while and afterwards it'll be as if nothing happened."

Meggie gestured weakly with the palm of her hand. "Maybe there was some confusion, perhaps she didn't say it was her birthday."

"Meggie, don't try and make excuses for her. There wasn't any misunderstanding. I know Jill, she's a lying cheat just like her mother was." The undisguised bitterness shocked Meggie.

She moved to the other side of the room, holding her arms around her middle protectively. "I feel terrible about the whole thing."

"It's not your fault," he insisted, the anger still evident in his voice. "God knows I've tried with Jill, but nothing seems to work."

"Quinn, no!" Meggie pleaded urgently. "Don't say things like that." She turned, her eyes meeting his, silently begging him to recognize Jill's unhappiness and all that was in the girl's life that was causing her to lie habitually.

"Oh, Meggie," he whispered huskily, pulling her into his arms. She laid her head on his firm shoulder as they held one another, not speaking, barely breathing. "I'm taking her back to her grandmother's," Quinn mumbled after a long time. "I don't think I'll be able to tolerate the sight of her for the rest of the weekend."

Meggie looked up, her eyes imploring. "Don't, for my sake. I want to settle this with Jill. I don't want either of us to brood about it for a whole week."

Indecision crossed over his face before he nodded curtly, "All right," he conceded.

After a restless night, Meggie called Quinn's about ten-thirty Sunday morning. Jill answered the phone.

"Hi, Jill," she greeted warmly. "I'm leaving for church in a few minutes and thought you might like to come along. Afterwards, if you like, we could stop at McDonald's and get a hamburger."

Jill hesitated. "I told you before I don't want to go to church. Besides I'm not hungry."

"Okay," Meggie sighed. It had been wrong to try to coax Jill into attending services with the promise of McDonald's, but Meggie was anxious for the opportunity to talk to her alone.

"Do you want me to tell Dad where you're at, so he won't start acting like a lunatic?" Jill questioned in a sarcastic tone.

"No," Meggie swallowed tightly. "I'm sure he'll figure it out." Defeated, she replaced the receiver and inhaled several deep breaths. She dressed in a crisp, romantic taffeta blouse and olive green skirt with a softly pleated front. Debating if she'd need her coat or not, she decided to take it. Just as she placed her hand on the doorknob the phone rang.

The first thought that raced through her mind

was that Jill had changed her mind. Meggie smiled to herself, thinking Jill had decided she'd rather attend church with her than spend an uncomfortable morning with her father.

"Hello," she answered cheerfully.

The muffled vulgarities jolted Meggie and she gave a small cry of alarm, slamming the phone down. It was the caller again. How could he have gotten her new number? All the blood rushed from her face as the room began to swim. With trembling legs she sank into the couch. "Why?" she whispered in a tormented prayer. "Why?"

It was several minutes before Meggie composed herself enough to stand. She breathed in deeply and with renewed determination and resolve, walked out the door.

Quinn was stepping off the elevator just as Meggie entered the building, a disgruntled look twisting his face.

"Quinn," she said softly, her hand reaching for his forearm.

He paused, the craggy features relaxing as his eyes met hers.

"He phoned again," she told him bluntly.

The trained eyes almost snapped with mental alertness. "What did he say?" Quinn demanded.

Meggie shook her head weakly. "The same . . . things."

"Did he threaten you?"

Again she shook her head. "I . . . I didn't listen long."

He ran his fingers through his hair. "Who has your new phone number?"

Meggie had asked herself the same question all the way home.

"My boss at Hadley," she told him, still deep in thought. "Carol Harris, one of the girls I work with." She bit into her bottom lip. "The apartment manager here . . . that's all. *You* don't even have my number." Although, she'd given it to Jill the day before. "How did *he* get it? Who could have given it to him?"

"I don't know." Quinn shook his head, inhaling an annoyed breath. "But this can't go on much longer." His mouth twisted slightly. "I want you to unplug your phone until this thing blows over."

Meggie shifted, avoiding his penetrating eyes. "I won't do that. What's the use of having a phone at all if I'm not going to be able to use it? Besides, it would worry my dad if he tried to phone and couldn't get me. I'm not going to let this creep ruin my life."

"Meggie, be reasonable," Quinn muttered harshly.

She smiled bravely, but her lips gave a telltale tremble. "I am reasonable. I sometimes think I'm the only sane person left in this world."

His gaze fell on her sweet, parted lips. "I'm beginning to think so, too," he said in a strange, deep voice. Tenderly his hand cupped her cheek. "I'll be gone for the next couple of hours. Jill's through sulking; you might be able to talk to her without me around."

Softly, her lips brushed the palm of his hand. "Don't worry about me. Jill and I will be fine."

Suddenly his eyes were smoldering as he searched her face. Unexpectedly he leaned forward, kissing her long and hard.

Dazed, Meggie watched him walk out of the building, following his diminishing figure until she couldn't see him any longer. A soft smile touched her lips and she raised a finger to her mouth, astonished that she could respond so fully to this one man, equally amazed at the flare of passion he was able to stir within her with one kiss.

It was several minutes before Meggie approached her apartment door. The key was in the lock when Jill stepped into the corridor.

"Hi," Jill mumbled, her eyes not quite meeting Meggie's.

"Jill," she said softly, hoping to show the girl she wasn't angry. "Have you decided when you'd like to have me give you a perm?"

A spark of excitement entered the blue eyes but was quickly concealed. She gave an uninterested shrug. "It doesn't matter, nothing's going to help my hair anyway."

"I could probably do something," Meggie said

confidently. "I've always had a knack with hair. We could trim some off here." She lifted Jill's bangs. "And add a little curl here." She tugged a strand from behind her ear. "And if we're really daring we could dye this side pink."

Jill smiled, slowly raising her eyes so they met Meggie's. "If it's all right, maybe we could do it today?"

"I'm not planning anything special," Meggie said as she turned the key, unlocking the front door. Jill followed her inside the apartment, and sat stiffly on the couch while Meggie changed clothes. When she returned from the bedroom, she noticed Jill was leafing through the Bible she'd set on the coffee table, her gaze intent as she turned the pages as if seeking to know what was inside that claimed such respect from Meggie. As soon as Jill realized that Meggie was present she laid the book aside with an indifferent air. "Ready?" She stood expectantly.

"We'll have to buy the perm. But there should be one at the grocery store. I need to pick up a few things besides."

"I bet that manager will make a play for you again," Jill said in a teasing tone. "I noticed the way he was looking at you last week."

"Jill!" Meggie said, stunned. "Ken was just being helpful."

"Oh sure," Jill said on a long sigh.

Almost from the time Meggie had moved into

the apartment complex she had done her weekly shopping at the local food store. Her first time there the manager, Ken Wallace, had introduced himself and helped her out with her groceries. Meggie hadn't read anything into his thoughtfulness. Ken was the friendly, outgoing type. She'd shopped there several times since, and Ken had always gone out of his way to say hello, but there had never been anything more than a friendly exchange of words between them.

When Meggie and Jill had gone shopping the week before, Ken had opened another cash register at the checkout stand and had personally rung up her groceries. They'd chatted but nothing more. Apparently Jill had read a lot more than there was into the exchange.

"I think you're off base this time, kid," Meggie said.

Jill snapped her head around. "I know a flirt when I see one," she protested.

Meggie momentarily closed her eyes at the angry outburst. Sometimes Jill was like a powder keg ready to explode.

When they entered the store, Ken waved a friendly hello.

"See what I mean?" Jill whispered with an I-told-you-so look flashing from her eyes.

Meggie returned Ken's greeting, but averted her eyes as she placed her purse in the cart and rounded the corner toward the produce section.

In a matter of only a few minutes, Meggie had collected the items she needed and was heading for the checkout stand when Ken called her.

"I'll help you over here." His friendly smile formed deep grooves in the lean, tan cheeks. Tall and blond, his good looks were an attraction many women shoppers wouldn't ignore.

"Thanks, Ken." Meggie smiled a little self-consciously as Jill eyed her knowingly.

After placing the items in brown bags, Ken accepted Meggie's check. "Is everything correct?" he questioned as he circled the informational portion of the check.

Nonplussed by Jill's glances and attitude, Meggie blurted out, "No, my phone number's been changed."

Practiced fingers recorded the new number at the top of the check. When he glanced up he gave her a bright smile. "I'll help you out with these."

"That's not necessary," Meggie said quickly. Jill was leaning against the counter, a thumb tucked into the loop of her jeans, a mocking smile twisting her mouth.

Ken handed Meggie the bag. "See you next week then."

"Good-bye, Ken, thanks," she murmured in an uncomfortable voice.

"See," Jill insisted with a smirk on the way out the door. "That guy's sweet on you." With an upward sweep of her chin she batted her eyelashes at Meggie innocently. "Don't be so naive, Meggie dear."

"Will you stop," Meggie snapped impatiently. "You're like a bulldog who's got a hold of something and won't let go."

Hurt and surprise showed in Jill's eyes and she closed her mouth, pressing her lips together until they formed a tight line. She didn't say another word the entire way home.

She sulked in the living room while Meggie put the groceries away. Several times Meggie paused, glancing into the other room where Jill was watching television. Letting out her breath slowly to calm her nerves, Meggie silently berated herself for reacting angrily to Jill's teasing. That was all it had been, she realized that now. Why should she expect a thirteen-year-old to behave like a mature adult? Jill was only acting her age. Meggie should have been more tolerant. By making a fuss she had inflicted another wound in Jill's already deflated ego.

She sauntered into the living room, the perm box in her hand. "Why don't you wash your hair while I read over the perm instructions," Meggie suggested after a bit.

Jill glanced away from the television and shrugged. Sluggishly she rose from the chair as if it required an extraordinary amount of effort and walked out of the apartment.

Ten minutes later she was back, a towel wrapped

around her head turban-style. Sitting at the kitchen table, Meggie looked up.

"I hope you're ready for this," she commented with a cheerful smile. "Remember I don't offer any guarantees. You could end up looking like Lassie."

Unconcerned, Jill sat in the chair opposite Meggie and slumped forward. "Even that would be an improvement."

Meggie smiled, unwrapping the towel from the girl's head. "Do you want me to trim off the ends a little?"

Jill's eyes met hers speculatively. "Whatever you think," she remarked without enthusiasm.

After running the comb through the long hair and carefully studying its texture, Meggie began working. She'd cut off about an inch of the blonde length and was putting the hair into tiny curlers when there was a sharp rap at the door.

Before Meggie could respond, Quinn walked boldly into the apartment. His eyes held an unfriendly light.

"I thought I told you to always keep this door locked. Phone calls or not, it's simple common sense these days."

Meggie opened and closed her mouth without saying a word. "Yes, Your Highness." She curtsied mockingly. She chose to make a joke of it, or would have reacted angrily.

The apartment door was always locked, it was

second nature to her; Jill had been the last one in the apartment. But Meggie gladly accepted the blame, rather than tell Quinn his daughter had left the door unlocked.

"Hi, Dad." The soft, young features smiled eagerly.

Quinn ignored Jill. "Don't laugh this off, Meggie. Promise me that from now on you'll keep the door locked . . . always."

Their eyes dueled, his dark ones sparking with anger, her softer ones indulging him.

"Meggie, I'm serious."

Her smile was tender when she nodded. "So am I. From now on I'll be sure it's locked."

The tension left his face, relaxing tiny lines around his sensuous mouth and eyes. "Is that coffee I smell?" His gaze rested on the pot which had just finished perking.

"Want a cup?" she asked, taking a mug from the cupboard even before he assured her he did.

Quinn sat opposite Jill eyeing the headful of pink and green curlers. His hands cupped the steaming mug. "I'm almost afraid to ask what you two are doing."

"Meggie's giving me a perm," Jill announced, her voice slightly high in her eagerness. "It's going to be like Meggie's."

Quinn raised his gaze until their eyes locked. Meggie found herself mesmerized by their unfathomable depths.

"Everything about Meggie, hair included, is certainly beautiful," he whispered with an odd catch in his voice.

Meggie dropped her eyes, her heart thundering at the potency of his words. If not for Jill's presence Meggie would have willingly slipped her arms around his neck, and hungrily sought his mouth. The chemistry between them was stronger than anything she had ever experienced in her life. Her heart was reaching out to this man. Never had any pull been more powerful.

"Ken thinks so, too," Jill said smugly.

"Ken?" Quinn riveted his attention on his daughter.

"Yeah, he's the guy from the grocery store who's out to get Meggie. Boy, Dad, you wouldn't believe how he went after her today. Meggie says it's all in my head, but I know a snow job when I see one," she finished with a half-chuckle.

Meggie turned, pouring herself a cup of coffee in an attempt to hold her temper. Jill was jealous. Meggie had seen it in her eyes when Quinn had ignored her and spoke to Meggie when he first arrived. Now she was making sure she received some attention.

"As I explained to Jill," Meggie said calmly, her voice soft and distinct to make every word clear, "Ken is the manager of the Maywood. He's been friendly and helpful, but he has no romantic interest in me."

"That's what she says," Jill spat.

Quinn seemed to ignore both comments, continuing to drink his coffee. His gaze was brooding as he studied the weather outside Meggie's lanai. "It looks like we're in for a bad storm. The sky is almost black."

Unconsciously Meggie released a short sigh of relief. Quinn knew his daughter and realized that Jill had probably greatly exaggerated the situation. A smile of thankfulness touched her soft mouth as she carefully applied the setting solution onto Jill's hair.

"The first weeks after I moved here from Los Angeles, I wondered if the sun ever made it through the heavy clouds in this section of the world. Talk about climate shock! We were having a mild winter in California. I had one heck of a cold sitting out the monsoons here." She laughed lightly. "Now a little rain doesn't bother me in the least. Portland . . . Oregon is so beautiful in so many other ways it doesn't matter."

Quinn grinned, seeming to agree with her growing appreciation for the Northwest.

"Have you thought about who has your new phone number?" he quizzed.

With a defeated shrug of her shoulder, Meggie shook her head. "There's no one else."

"Meggie gave Ken her phone number today." Jill cast her father a look of complete angelic innocence.

Meggie locked her hands in front of her as she witnessed Quinn's reaction.

"Is that true?" he demanded.

"Of course, it's true," Jill insisted. "I promised you I'd only tell the truth from now on. You've got to believe me, Dad."

"I'll ask Meggie," Quinn shot back, his eyes locking with hers. "I want a simple yes or no. Did you or did you not give this Ken your phone number?"

Meggie's soft brown eyes pleaded with him. "Quinn, let me explain."

"Just answer the question."

Folding her arms around her middle as if to ward off a chill, Meggie nodded.

"She's meeting him for dinner tonight. She didn't think I was listening when they made the arrangements, but I heard everything," Jill continued maliciously, apparently pleased with the reaction she was receiving from her father with this bit of information.

"Is that true?" One thick brow rose questioningly.

"Would it matter if it was or not?" Meggie demanded defiantly. Not once did she flinch under his discerning gaze. The silence between them gnawed at her heart, but she held her head proud, her posture rigid.

"I guess there's not much more to say then, is there?" he asked. The lack of emotion in his voice made the words all the more final.

Tears stung the back of her eyes, but Meggie met his look evenly, not giving him the satisfaction of knowing what he was doing to her. When he stood there was a weary droop to his shoulders. Meggie had to fight back a denial, to cry out and stop him, to beg him to trust her.

He didn't say a word as he walked across the room. His hand was on the doorknob when he turned, his dark eyes cutting and cruel.

"I thought you were different."

Meggie could feel her heart shatter into a million infinitesimal pieces as Quinn walked out of the apartment.

The closing door made a quiet clicking noise and Meggie thought she had never heard anything louder. It was as if Quinn was closing off all communication between them. The vibrating sound seemed to fill the room.

"Why did you do that?" Meggie demanded, acid tears stinging her face. Her hand closed around the back of the chair until her fingers were white.

"Do what?" Jill asked innocently. "I only told Dad the truth. You did give Ken your phone number and I heard him say he'd be seeing you."

Her mouth felt suddenly dry, her throat parched. Nervously she moistened her lips. Angry tension was knotting her stomach. "You did that purposely. This was the one way you could get back at me because your dad found out you'd lied about it being your birthday."

"That's not true," Jill shouted. "I never said it was my birthday, you misunderstood me. But dad doesn't believe *me*."

Meggie's chin tilted proudly; she had only been guessing at the extent of Jill's anger. Now the desire to retaliate was clear in the vindictive blue eyes. The look shocked Meggie and she swallowed the hard lump forming in her throat.

It didn't matter to Jill whom she was hurting, or what her lies would do to the relationship between Meggie and her father. That sparked a burning anger within Meggie. She had always had a problem with her temper, but now it raged.

Jill gave a gasping cry of hurt and surprise as Meggie began ripping the tiny curlers from the blonde head.

"Ouch . . . stop." Jill's hands flew to her head protectively but Meggie slapped them aside.

"I may have plenty of things wrong with me but my ears aren't one of them. I abhor liars," she spat, yanking one curler out after the other. "I hate them so much I refuse to have anything to do with them and that includes giving perms."

"Stop! You're hurting me," Jill cried.

"Good," Meggie returned, "maybe then you'll understand what your lies do to others." Within seconds the blonde hair was free, falling about the pale face in wet ringlets. Jill's shoulders began to shake.

Forcibly, Meggie's fingers closed over the chin,

raising it to look into her eyes. "Do you think you're fooling anyone with your lies? Do you?" she demanded.

Numbly Jill shook her head. Tears were brimming in the blue depths.

The show of emotion didn't stop Meggie. "Do you think you're going to impress me by making up all these untruths? You're not." She inhaled deeply at the look of shock in Jill's pale features.

"I hate you." Each word was spat with intensity as Jill stood in front of Meggie, small hands clenched at her side.

It had been a long time since Meggie had allowed her temper to rage like this. "Go ahead and hate me, but I'll always like you."

With a dignity that surprised Meggie, Jill walked across the room. "I won't bother you again," she said in a choked whisper and slipped through the door.

Meggie's fingers were trembling as she placed a hand over her mouth. Her legs didn't feel steady as she pulled out a chair and sat down. Closing her eyes did little to relieve the throbbing ache that was building at her temple.

"Stupid Meggie," she muttered brokenly. Again and again she'd wrestled with her temper. Her father claimed it was the Irish blood that flowed in her veins, but that was only an excuse and a flimsy one at best. So much for showing Jill and Quinn an example of Christian love, God's love.

A half-hour later, Meggie didn't feel any better. She knew the only thing that would ease this knot of tension in her stomach was to apologize to Jill and attempt to undo some of the damage.

She paused, praying for wisdom and strength before picking up the phone. Quinn answered.

"I'm sorry to bother you," she said awkwardly. "But can I talk to Jill for a minute?"

"Jill?" he returned after a short pause. "I thought she was with you."

"No." A sinking sensation came over Meggie. "We had a fight and I . . . I told her to . . . oh, Quinn, where could she be?"

A grimness sounded in his voice. "I wouldn't worry. When something troubles Jill, she usually runs to her grandmother. I'll phone Hariette and get back to you."

Meggie paced the floor waiting for the phone to ring. The second it sounded, she jerked it off the hook. "Yes?"

"Hariette hasn't heard from her."

"Oh no, I was afraid of something like this. She's run away and it's my fault," Meggie said in a tortured whisper.

"I'll be right over."

The dial tone buzzed in her ear; still Meggie continued to hold the phone, her mind racing through channels that were too frightening to investigate.

The sharp rap at the door broke Meggie from the

fearful stupor and she bolted upright and opened the door.

"What happened?" he demanded. "What did you say to her?"

Meggie blinked back tears and shook her head. "I lost my temper, I told her the lies weren't fooling me. Jill said she hated me. I pulled the curlers out of her hair. . . ." She didn't finish, hanging her head, unwilling to see the look of contempt in his eyes. She could feel the heat flooding color up her neck and face. It was difficult to breathe, to think.

"She must have decided to walk back to Hariette's," Quinn murmured thoughtfully.

Meggie gasped as she looked out the window. The storm had broken and the rain was coming down in angry torrents, sheet after sheet pelting the earth with a vengeance. "I'll never forgive myself if anything happens to her." She rushed to the closet and grabbed a jacket. "We've got to find her."

Quinn took the car keys from his pants pocket and nodded, a pinched look about his mouth.

Driving around, up and down every block proved pointless. No one was out in the storm, even the streets were deserted. Visibility was extremely poor and Meggie strained her eyes as the windshield wipers beat furiously against the front window.

"There," she cried, pointing to a park bench in

a small grassy area off one of the side streets.

Quinn leaned forward, squinting. "That's not her."

"I'm going to look." Even before he could protest, Meggie was out of the car. She gasped at the force of the rain as it hit her. The bitter wind whipped the coat from her body and she struggled with the sash at the waist. But the thin material offered little protection and she was soaked to the skin almost immediately. Unconcerned, Meggie raced across the streets to the small park. But Quinn was right; whoever, or whatever, had been there was gone.

Her head down, Meggie made her way back to Quinn, but when she came to the sidewalk where she'd left the car, he too was gone. She looked around helplessly and shivered. Rivulets of rain rolled down her back; her clothes were plastered to her body. She was blocks from the apartment and there was no one in sight.

Chapter Six

Meggie had never felt so hot. Kicking the covers away with her foot, she rolled onto her back, laying her forearm across her eyes. Her throat felt as if it was on fire and every swallow was agony. The bedside clock told her it was 2:00 A.M. Slowly her eyes closed. At least Jill was safe and that was all that mattered.

After Meggie had jumped out of the Jeep, Quinn had seen his daughter taking shelter from the storm in the doorway of a local business. He'd picked her up and then gone back for Meggie, but had been unable to locate her. Since Hariette's was only a few blocks from where he was, Quinn had driven Jill to her grandmother's and gone back, looking for Meggie. He found her a block from the apartment building. Although drenched and shivering, Meggie was more concerned that Quinn had found Jill. Her relief could hardly be expressed with words.

She'd taken a hot bath and crawled into bed. But it didn't seem to matter how many blankets she piled on, she couldn't get warm. Now she felt as if she was in the same room as a blast furnace; the sweat was pouring off her.

Shivering, Meggie woke again at seven with the alarm. She reached for the covers and curled into a tight ball to chase away the sudden chill. At seven-fifteen she forced herself out of bed. The room spun crazily and she sat down, slowly lowering herself onto the mattress. It took several minutes before she felt strong enough to stand again. She placed her hands against the wall, using it as a support in case she felt faint. By the time she reached the kitchen, she was trembling.

Pouring herself a small glass of apple juice from the refrigerator, she took down the aspirin bottle from the cupboard. The childproof cap wouldn't twist open and Meggie felt like crying. Who would have believed opening a simple bottle would take so much effort? Her hands were shaking almost uncontrollably as she shook two tablets into the palm of her hand.

The aspirin had begun to dissolve in her mouth by the time she lifted the cold juice to her lips. It was agony to swallow, but somehow she downed the medication. Phoning the office to say she was sick and wouldn't be in was another task that drained her of reserved strength. Her boss was reassuring and told her to get well and not to worry about the office.

Meggie almost fell back into bed. Immediately she drifted into a dreamless slumber. The next time she opened her eyes it was afternoon. She felt moderately better and forced herself to swallow more aspirin and drink another glass of juice. Taking the pillow from her bed she lay down on the davenport and turned on the television.

Feeling considerably worse by evening, Meggie spent the night on the couch. It required too much effort to force herself to return to her bedroom. When she phoned the office Tuesday morning, she was again assured everything was fine. She replaced the receiver, shocked at how weak and strained her voice sounded.

The aspirin remained on the end table with a pitcher of juice and Meggie forced herself to drink liquids, but nothing seemed to help the raging fire in her throat.

That afternoon the doorbell chimed. Meggie glanced at the front door, wondering if she had the strength to answer the repeated knock. She struggled into a sitting position as the room spun wildly around her.

By leaning heavily against the door frame, Meggie was able to stand upright.

"You look awful." Concern knitted Quinn's brow into furrowed lines.

"Thanks." She attempted a feeble smile.

Quinn jerked his fingers through his tawny hair as he studied her. "I wondered when I didn't see you the past couple of mornings if you were sick. I'm glad I decided to check." With a supporting arm around her shoulders he helped her back to the sofa. Gently he brushed away the limp hair from her face. His hand felt refreshingly cool against her skin and she closed her eyes.

"You're burning with fever."

"I'm all right," she insisted weakly. "I'm better today."

Quinn didn't sound convinced. "What did you feel like *yesterday?*"

The slight quiver of her lips was a poor imitation of a smile. "Rotten."

His mouth curved up cynically, adding a harshness to the craggy features. "If there's not a vast improvement in your condition by tomorrow, I'm taking you to the doctor."

Meggie forced her eyes open. "No," she protested. "I'll be okay. I just need some rest, that's all."

Before she could protest, she was gently lifted into the air, one arm behind her knees, the other supporting her back. Cradled in Quinn's arms she felt safe and protected and laid her head against his shoulder, smiling softly to herself.

With great care he placed her on the mattress and removed the slippers from her feet. When she slipped out of the velour robe, Quinn laid it at the foot of the bed.

"What—no wet cloth across my forehead? The very least you could do is hold my hand and whisper soothingly."

For the first time that afternoon Quinn smiled. Meggie glanced away for fear the look in her eyes would betray her feelings.

"Can I get you anything before I go?"

It hurt so much to talk that Meggie simply shook her head.

"I'll be back later. I'm taking the apartment key from your purse so you won't have to get up and answer the door. Okay?"

Meggie's lips trembled with a smile. Lying back with her head supported by the pillow, she heard him leave. The sound of the door locking was comforting and she closed her eyes, knowing Quinn would return.

"Meggie?" Someone was calling to her from a far distance, but she didn't know where. Weights seemed to be holding her eyes shut. She was sick, so sick. Never could she remember feeling this awful.

"Meggie, it's Quinn. Can you hear me?" The softly spoken words were issued close to her ear.

She gave a tiny nod.

"I'm taking you to the hospital."

She tried to protest, but all her effort resulted in nothing but a pitiful moan. Lifelessly her head fell back as a muscled arm lifted her from the bed. She was carried only a short distance and set down. Quinn took her limp arms, inserting them into the sleeves of her coat. Meggie tried to help but the simple function was beyond her.

There was little about the ride to the hospital that stayed in her mind. Worried glances from Quinn, soft assurances at every stoplight. Her one thought was how good the cold air felt against her burning skin.

Quinn carried her inside the emergency room and laid her gently on one of the examining tables. A doctor's kind eyes stared down at her, momentarily blocking out the bright light that blinded her. Quinn was standing by her side holding one hand.

"I'm taking a culture, but I can just about guarantee it's streptococci."

"Strep throat?" Quinn questioned in a worried voice. "Will she be all right?"

The sound of their voices drifted away, but Meggie heard the doctor telling Quinn she'd need heavy doses of antibiotics, and someone to look after her. Meggie wanted to say she didn't need anyone, she could take care of herself, when Quinn assured the physician that he'd be taking care of her.

The next thing Meggie knew she was back in her own bed. The room was dark and she rolled her head to look at the clock. It was after six. Shadows from the rising sun flitted across the walls and she raised herself up on one elbow to find Quinn slouched in a chair on the opposite side of the small room. He was asleep, his frame filling the chair. Forearms were crisscrossed over his chest while his head was tilted to one side, half resting on his shoulder.

Meggie's brown eyes drank in the sight of him. For once she could look at him, watch the gentle rise and fall of his chest without the fear of his reading the love in her eyes. His face was relaxed in slumber, the aquiline profile less sharp. Studying him stirred something deep within her breast. Meggie yearned to reach out and touch him.

Quinn must have felt her quiet appraisal because his eyes leisurely opened and met hers. For a long time he didn't move, their eyes speaking the words that had never been verbalized. The undisguised tenderness robbed her lungs of oxygen and she extended her hand, reaching out to him.

Unfolding his arms, Quinn stood, his eyes smiling deeply into hers.

"You look awful," she whispered.

Taking her fingers, he smiled down at her mockingly. "Now that's the pot calling the kettle black. Taken a look in the mirror lately?"

Meggie shook her head, glancing away embarrassed. It didn't take much of an imagination to know what she must look like. She needed a bath, her hair was a mass of tangles. But for the first time in days her throat wasn't a consuming fire and she felt that she could drink something.

Quinn kissed her fingertips as if she were a delicate flower and knelt beside her, resting his elbows on the bed. "It doesn't matter what you look like. To me you'll always be beautiful."

Tears pricked her eyes as her hand lovingly

investigated the rugged lines of his face, enjoying the feel of his unshaven skin against the sensitive palm of her hand.

A muscle jerked in the side of his jaw as he stopped her action, gripping her hand securely between his two larger ones.

"Do you feel like you might be able to eat something?" he asked.

Food didn't interest her and she shook her head. "I'm thirsty."

A feather-light kiss brushed her brow. "I'll be back in a jiffy."

By the time he returned, Meggie was sitting up and Quinn handed her a tall frosted glass. It looked like a milkshake, but she didn't ask. It was still painful to swallow, but the liquid felt cold and soothing against the back of her throat.

Pulling the chair closer to the bed, Quinn sat beside her, leaning forward so his elbows rested on his knees.

"How's Jill?" Meggie managed to ask in a hoarse whisper.

The thick brows came together in a heavy scowl. "Fine." His response was clipped, almost angry. "It's her fault you're sick."

Meggie's fingers bit into his arm. "No," she said quickly and winced at the pain in her throat. "What happened to me is my own doing. I lost my temper. I don't blame Jill for running away."

His gaze narrowed, his eyes avoiding hers. "As

far as I'm concerned this whole thing happened because of Jill, but we'll talk about it later. Right now let's concentrate on getting you well."

"But, Quinn," she pleaded.

Long fingers covered her lips. "No buts. Do you feel strong enough to take a bath?"

Meggie nodded eagerly.

"I'll run the water. You can bathe alone but I insist you leave the door unlocked in case you need me." The alarm must have shown in her eyes. "I'm not going to come rushing in unless it's absolutely necessary. You'll have to trust me, Meggie."

She glanced longingly toward the bathroom and shrugged, lifting her palms in a gesture of defeat. What else was there to do but trust him?

Crow's-feet crinkled the laugh lines about his eyes. "You want me to add bath salts or any of that other stuff you women like?"

Meggie flushed and Quinn laughed. Gently he guided her into the bathroom and set her on the seat while he prepared the water, adding the scented salts.

There was never a bath Meggie had enjoyed more. True, she felt weak and shaky, but she lay back luxuriating in the feel of water against her aching muscles. She felt like she'd just completed running a marathon and was sore in spots she barely knew existed.

After combing her hair and brushing her teeth

she felt like a new woman. Quinn was changing the sheets on her bed when she entered the bedroom. Meggie paused, leaning against the door frame, watching him as he worked.

"You'd make a wonderful maid," she teased, her voice low and slightly husky.

Quinn swiveled around, his head tilted mockingly. "I should have known you wouldn't let this pass without comment." He lifted back the covers for her. "Now come to bed like a good girl." He fluffed up the pillows. As soon as she was tucked in, Quinn sat on the edge of the bed. "I've got to get ready for work. Will you be all right by yourself?"

She reassured him with a warm smile and a slight shake of her head.

A masculine hand slid beneath the long hair at the back of her neck, pressing her forward into the wall of his chest. He held her to him as if she was the most precious, the most delicate being in all the world. The fingers of one hand gently massaged her back while the other entwined with her hair.

Meggie closed her eyes to the heady delight of being in his embrace. Her heart seemed to beat in a gentle drum roll and she wondered fleetingly if he could hear and feel what his touch did to her.

His breath stirred the hair at the side of her face. "Are you sure you'll be okay?" The gentle concern in his voice nearly stopped her heart.

"Don't worry about me."

Again he ran his hand down the length of her hair, letting it rest on the gentle curve of her shoulder. "I can't help but be concerned. At least I had sense enough to check on you when I didn't see you two mornings in a row." He paused as if lost in some private hell.

"Quinn?" Her hand reached for his.

He gave a short shake of his head. "I'll be back at lunchtime. Rest until then. Understood?"

"Yes, master," she murmured teasingly. "Can we talk about Jill then?"

He regarded her seriously, then nodded. "If that's what you want."

She wasn't tired and the morning passed slowly. Now that she was taking the antibiotics, her throat had quit hurting, the fever had broken and she felt almost human again. Several times she thought about getting dressed, but didn't want to push things; she was still incredibly weak.

As promised, Quinn returned about noon, carrying a sack with a restaurant's name printed on the front.

"Hi." The greeting was made in a small voice as Meggie sat up in bed. She'd washed and styled her hair and felt reasonably attractive for him. "I hope something's in there for me. I'm starved."

Playfully, he placed the bag behind his back. "Not on your life, sister. This is my lunch."

Meggie widened her eyes dramatically. "I can

129

read the headlines now: 'Defenseless Woman Starves under Inspector's Care.'"

Lowering his frame onto the chair beside the bed, Quinn sighed. "In that case, I'd best share." Meggie had expected hamburgers, but Quinn brought out two large styrofoam cups and plastic spoons and handed one of each to her. "A cook friend of mine made the soup. I told him you were sick and he insisted this will cure anything." He took off the protective plastic cover and dipped the spoon inside.

The aroma of noodles and chicken swamped her senses and Meggie breathed in appreciatively. Quinn waited until she'd taken her mouthful before commenting.

"Good?"

Meggie rolled her eyes heavenward. "Nectar from the gods."

"I thought you Christians professed belief in only one God," he remarked drily.

Meggie stopped, the spoon lifted halfway to her mouth. "I do . . . that's only an expression."

His hand gave her leg a gentle squeeze. "I was only teasing."

Meggie lowered her gaze, chagrined. She was being overly defensive. Christ and her faith in Him were the most important things in her life. It was vital that Quinn share this faith if their relationship was to develop into something deep and permanent.

The soup was only half gone when Meggie set it aside, unable to eat any more.

"Done?" Quinn looked surprised.

Meggie shook her head and leaned against the pillow. "Would it be possible for me to talk to Jill soon?" she asked. "I'm not going to feel right until I've apologized."

Quinn's eyes darkened. "What do *you* have to apologize for? Jill was up to her tricks again, lying through her teeth. You don't owe her a thing."

Staring back at him with sad, disbelieving eyes, Meggie reached for his hand. "It wasn't all lies. I guess I owe you both an apology," she admitted humbly. "You've been so concerned about the caller that's been pestering me and I've been handing out my phone number every time I write a check without even thinking about it. Jill was telling you the truth when she said I'd given my number to Ken, but certainly not for personal reasons. I'm not likely to date him when there's someone else I care about." She hadn't meant to admit quite that much and quickly averted her eyes.

"That guy from Los Angeles," he growled, his mouth thinning with impatience while he made busy work of placing the leftovers in the sack.

Meggie's hand stopped his action, her eyes searching his. Could it possibly be he didn't know? Never had anyone been able to create such a response within her. Quinn had attracted her

131

even before they met. Meggie had never been the flirting type; she was incapable of being anything but open and honest about her feelings.

"It's you, Quinn, you must know that," she said softly.

The words held him motionless. "Me?" he drawled the question. Amazement flickered fleetingly across his face. "You care about me?" he questioned as if it was a ridiculous conjecture. "Listen, kid, don't waste your time on me, you'd be better off marrying the boyfriend you left behind." He stood, towering above her, his voice clipped and abrupt. "I was only being neighborly. I didn't mean for you to take any of this seriously."

The harshness in his voice was like daggers piercing her heart. Why did she have to be so ingenuous and unsophisticated? Quinn wasn't interested in her devotion; it embarrassed him. He had only been kind to her out of a sense of duty because of Jill. She had read so much more into it.

Meggie turned her face toward the wall, her lips trembling. "Thanks for lunch," she said, her voice barely audible. She couldn't see Quinn but she sensed his hesitancy. His piercing gaze seemed to reach out and touch her. Although her face was averted, she closed her eyes, refusing to allow him to see any of her pain.

"I'll be back tonight," he said after a while, his voice regretful, gentle.

Meggie wanted to tell him not to bother, she didn't need him anymore, but was afraid if she spoke her voice might crack and she'd make a bigger fool of herself.

For a long time after he'd gone, Meggie stared at the blank wall, her thoughts confused. Quinn was capable of very deep feelings. She had hoped, almost desperately, that he could come to care for her. A tear slipped from thick lashes; Meggie wiped it away with a sense of pride. She wouldn't mention her feelings again. The next move would have to come from him.

A nap took up a portion of the afternoon. A noise woke her and Meggie opened her eyes to find Jill standing uncomfortably in the bedroom doorway. The young forehead was creased in apprehension.

"Hi, Meggie," she said tightly, her fists doubled at her sides. "Dad said you were real sick and wanted to talk to me."

Meggie struggled to a sitting position and yawned. "I'm not on my deathbed, Jill, relax."

"Are you still real sick? I mean I could come back later if you wanted me to." The girl looked so ill at ease that Meggie couldn't avoid smiling.

"I'm fine," she assured the girl. "Come over and sit by me," she said, patting the edge of the bed.

Jill crossed the room with the eagerness of a condemned man and sat in the chair instead. Her folded hands rested on her lap like a model student.

"I'm pleased you could come, Jill. I wanted to talk to you and apologize."

"Apologize?" Jill repeated disbelievingly.

"I lost my temper. I'm sorry I pulled the curlers out of your hair; that must have hurt. If you give me another chance we could do the perm again."

"But I told Dad those things about you. You should have been angry with me and when I said I hated you . . . you said you'd always like me." Her eyes didn't quite meet Meggie's. She blinked, lowering her gaze.

"Perhaps I had a right to get angry, but there was certainly a better way of handling the situation."

Eyes as round as saucers set in a pale face stared down at the bed covers. It was so unusual to see Jill subdued that Meggie risked another statement. "I had trouble with my temper like you have trouble telling lies."

Jill nodded. "But you hardly ever get mad." The words sounded like they'd been squeezed out through a lump in her throat.

"That's not the way I used to be. Anything could set me off and I'd fly into a rage over the silliest things. I didn't have many friends and any I did have I'd lose the minute I lost my temper."

Jill chanced an incredulous glance at Meggie. "How'd you change?"

"Jesus helped me."

The young mouth twisted skeptically. "Oh sure, and how'd He do that?"

134

"I asked Him to," Meggie explained simply. "I tried to be different so many times. I hated myself every time I blew up unreasonably, but I couldn't seem to stop. No matter what I did, or how hard I tried, I couldn't hold on to my temper." She paused. "Then one day I raged at my only friend because she'd moved something of mine. I'd done poorly on a test and was angry at myself, not Jacquie, but I took out my frustration on her. I don't think I'll ever forget the look of horror in her eyes as I started throwing things around the room. Jacquie was so calm, so reasonable, and that angered me all the more. Finally she said that we'd talk after I'd settled down. With that she left the room. I knew then that I'd probably lost the only real friend I'd ever had." Meggie swallowed; she hadn't meant to talk so much and her throat was beginning to ache. But Jill was waiting expectantly for her to continue. "After Jacquie left the room, I sat down and cried. I was miserable, I was a college junior and was behaving like a two-year-old. I hated myself. Later Jacquie and I had a long talk and she told me about Jesus and that He could help me control my terrible temper. She made it sound so simple, that Christ was willing to help me change."

"It sounds too easy, I mean did you just say, 'Okay, Jesus, I want to change' and zap—you were different?" Jill asked anxiously.

"No." Meggie took a deep breath. "There were plenty of times that I blew it, especially in the beginning. But one day I was walking in the park and was watching a young mother with her baby. The child was about a year old and was attempting to walk. She'd take a couple of steps and plop down on her little bottom. Then she'd get up and try again. The whole time the mother was squatting down to the baby's level, holding her hands out, encouraging the child. Suddenly I knew that's how Christ saw me and my temper. Not once did that mother say, 'You big dummy, you really did it this time.' No! She was encouraging, reassuring her child. That was how Jesus was looking at me."

A hurt, pained look stole into Jill's expression. "I don't want to lie," she confessed openly, "but I do it all the time." She paused. "Do you think I could change?"

Meggie smiled gently. "I know who can help."

Jill spent several hours with Meggie, eager to wait on her. She even cooked Meggie's dinner and created her very own original omelette. Meggie ate what she could, praising her effort. Jill stayed as long as she dared without worrying her grandmother.

Later, after the sun had set and the room grew dark, Meggie lay back against the pillow feeling almost jubilant. Even if Quinn rejected her love she couldn't help but feel a sense of exhilaration after the afternoon with Jill. The girl reminded Meggie more and more of herself at thirteen.

Meggie didn't know how she got there, but she was in a bank. Repeatedly she tried to explain to the banker that she had been ill and that was the reason she hadn't deposited the check. The banker's face quickly became distorted, growing horns and an evil look. He stared at Meggie and laughed viciously. She screamed in terror. She didn't know this man, had never seen him before. He was the one who'd been making the obscene calls. Now he was trying to kill her and she was so weak, so sick and couldn't fight him off. She cried out again, thinking she would die. Suddenly Quinn was there and the evil man threw her aside. Meggie crashed into the wall, crying out for Quinn to be careful because the man had a gun. But it was too late and Quinn slumped to the floor, blood oozing between his fingers as he held his stomach.

"Meggie, Meggie." Someone was shaking her hard. Her eyes flew open to find Quinn standing above her. With a whimpering cry of relief she sat up and hugged him as if her very life depended on the hold.

"Thank God you're safe." Tears glistened in her eyes. The nightmare had been so real, so vivid. For Quinn to be there was like having him come back from the dead. "I dreamed you'd been killed," she told him, her voice shaking uncontrollably.

A short, breathy laugh slipped from his throat as his arms cradled her against the hard, muscular chest.

"It's going to take a lot more than a nightmare to do me in," he whispered in a soothing voice.

Needing assurance, her hands reached up to trace the outline of his face, gliding over each imposing, each ruggedly carved feature.

A hand captured hers, squeezing it tightly. Creating a short space between them, Quinn held her away so their eyes could meet in the dark. Meggie's tongue nervously moistened her lips. Quinn's gaze narrowed on the slightly parted mouth and a smoldering light flickered in his eyes.

"Meggie, oh, Meggie." The sound of her name was an odd mixture of regret and hunger as though he couldn't help himself. His mouth closed fiercely over hers and the rush of fire that spread over her had nothing to do with a fever or having been sick.

Instinctively Meggie opened her mouth to him, her lips trembling softly under the domineering possession. Again and again their lips met, each contact more potent than the one before. No longer were his kisses urgent, but a long series of sweet, drugged responses as though Quinn couldn't get enough of her.

"This is insane." With a groaning effort, he dragged his mouth from her, his breath jagged. He shuddered slightly and began to pull away, but Meggie stopped him. Hands on either side of his face cupping the masculine jaw, she brought his mouth back to hers. The resistance was only fleeting as Quinn groaned, his mouth capturing hers again.

Meggie's thoughts were chaotic. His touch dispelled all reason, producing a wildfire of longing deep within her heart. She couldn't bear it if he were to push her away. Not now, not ever.

"Meggie," he pleaded with a sighing moan. "We're playing with fire."

"Fire," she agreed, smiling up at him softly. "I've been sick, I'm too weak to resist."

His hard mouth closed over hers again, reigniting the flames of passion. "I'm weak too," he whispered huskily, speaking against her lips. "But either we stop now, or there are going to be two of us in that bed."

"Oh, Quinn," she moaned softly. He'd said that for shock value, to pull her back into reality. But when she looked at him, his rugged face bathed in the moonlight, Meggie was shocked. There was a deep intensity in his face. He hadn't been teasing; he was dead serious.

Sighing deeply, she laid her head upon his chest, comforted by the uneven thud of his heart.

"You're acting mighty brave," he repeated, his

large hands caressing the length of her arms in a sweeping motion as he half-sat across the top of her bed.

"I'm sorry my nightmare woke you," she whispered.

"I was sleeping on your couch," he murmured, his lips very gently caressing the top of her head as though the fresh smell of her hair was an intoxicant.

"Sleeping on *my* couch?" That surprised her. "Why?" She pulled away until their eyes met again in the dim light.

"I came over to talk to you about Jill," he explained, a pinched look twisting his mouth, "but you were already asleep and I didn't want to wake you. You've been so ill, I decided to play it safe and spend another night here in case you needed something."

"What about Jill?" Meggie questioned, concerned.

Quinn stiffened and ran his hands wearily over his face. "Listen, Meggie, I don't want to offend you. Each of us is entitled to our own beliefs. But don't go filling Jill's head with this phony religion."

Chapter Seven

"Y ou're not staying late again, are you?" Carol Harris questioned with a worried glance.

Meggie looked up and feigned a cheerful smile. A large stack of policies bordered two sides of her desk. "I have to if I want to get caught up."

"But, Meggie, you were really sick; you missed all of last week. No one expects you to make up the entire workload by staying late every night. You'll only make yourself ill again." The petite blonde with pale blue eyes glanced over the piles of work that needed to be finished. "I'd stay with you," she volunteered with a guilty look, "but I've got a date with John tonight."

"Don't worry about it," Meggie told her friend. "I'm not going to be too much longer." Her elbows were resting on an open policy.

"Can I get you anything before I go?" Carol offered.

"A cup of coffee," Meggie told her gratefully.

A while later when Meggie lifted the plastic cup to her mouth, the last drops of cold coffee surprised her and she glanced at the clock. It was after seven and her stomach reminded her with a growl that she hadn't eaten since lunchtime.

Flexing the tired muscles of her shoulders, she leaned against the back of the chair and yawned.

After two late nights this week Meggie was exhausted. Yet working overtime didn't seem to be decreasing the number of policies on her desk. As hard as she worked to catch up during regular work hours, several stacks remained on her desk. Eyeing one last pile, she promised herself she'd quit once they were finished.

The sound of shoes clicking against the polished linoleum floor surprised her and she turned around.

"Quinn." Her eyes rounded with pleased excitement.

The angry intensity of his look burst the bubble of pleasure seeing him had created.

How did he get inside the building? The security men were well trained and wouldn't let just anyone inside at night. One of the older guards, George, had escorted Meggie to her car the night before, declaring it wasn't safe for a woman to be on the streets alone at night. It wasn't likely they'd allow someone in simply because Quinn claimed to know her.

"What are you doing?" he demanded, ignoring her greeting.

"Working," Meggie supplied, mystified as much by his attitude as by his presence.

"At this hour? I thought you went home at five."

"Yes, normally, but I've got to catch up with all this." Her hand made a sweeping motion over her desk.

His hand reached out, pulling her to her feet. "Come on, you're going home."

"Quinn?" She jerked herself free. "What's gotten into you? You're acting like a madman. I'm working a few hours late, so what?"

"So what?" he growled back at her. "I didn't spend a miserable week as your nursemaid so you could work yourself into a relapse. Is that understood?"

"No, it's not," she shot back angrily. "What gives you the right to dictate what I can and what I cannot do?"

The dark eyes narrowed to a menacing frown. "Two wretched nights sleeping in a chair," he responded tightly. "Get your coat, I'm taking you home."

Eyes flashing fire, and arms akimbo, Meggie shook her head. "No, you're not."

"Don't bet on it, lady."

"I wouldn't argue with the man, Miss O'Halloran." An amused voice spoke from behind her.

Meggie swiveled around to find the security guard who'd walked her to her car the night before.

"Evening, George," Quinn said pleasantly.

"Donnelley." George nodded, a maze of wrinkles creasing his face as he smiled. "It won't do you any good to argue with one of Portland's finest detectives, miss. My advice is to let him take you home."

Meggie wanted to snap that she wasn't particularly interested in his advice, but she bit back the words.

"This yours?" Quinn asked, holding up the pale peach-colored jacket.

Thwarted, Meggie nodded tersely. With her mouth pinched shut, she grabbed the jacket out of his hand and took her purse from the bottom desk drawer.

"Good night, George," she murmured in a strained voice. "I'll see you tomorrow evening. I'll be working late to make up for what I couldn't do tonight."

"No, she won't," Quinn contradicted her sternly. After a curt nod to George, he followed Meggie across the huge open floor.

Rather than wait for the elevator, Meggie took the stairs. The echo of Quinn's purposeful steps directly behind her only quickened her pace. Marching through the accounting department, Meggie made her way toward the employees' parking lot in the back of the building.

"Meggie, stop," Quinn insisted.

She tossed him an irritated glance over her shoulder and continued out of the building. Before she reached her car an abrupt hand on her arm whirled her around.

"Meggie, would you stop; I want to talk to you," Quinn demanded tensely.

"No," she snapped. "What gives you the right to

come here and treat me like a ten-year-old?" Her voice cracked and she turned away, attempting to steady her breath.

She hadn't seen Quinn in days. Jill hadn't been over that weekend and Meggie could only surmise that Quinn had prevented the girl from visiting. That hurt. He may not have approved of her "phony religion," as he called it, but to purposely keep Jill away was like saying he didn't trust Meggie. That hurt more.

His eyes were flashing fire, but he dropped his hand and let her go. "I wanted to arrange for a tracer on your phone, but we'll talk when you're in a more reasonable frame of mind."

"You'll have a long wait, Quinn Donnelley," she informed him heatedly.

An hour later Meggie paced the carpeted floor of her apartment, arms folded across her chest. She sank down in one of the living room chairs, only to jerk herself upright a minute later. At least she hadn't completely lost her cool. The line between anger and rage with Meggie could be thin and she was grateful to have escaped when she did. Past experience had taught her that if she paused, read through a few psalms, she would feel better. Meggie reached for her Bible.

They met at the elevator the next morning. Meggie had left a few minutes later than usual in hopes of missing Quinn, but he was there almost as if he'd been waiting for her.

"Good morning, Meggie." His smile was bright and cheerful.

Meggie had slept restlessly and wasn't in any mood to exchange banter with him. Rather than say anything at all she nodded curtly and punched the button for the bottom floor with unnecessary force. The elevator doors closed slowly.

"You don't look well," Quinn continued on a cheerful note. "Didn't you get enough sleep last night? You're looking thinner too." When she didn't respond to either statement, he proceeded further. "It's probably those late hours you've been keeping lately," he said with a knowing look.

The minute the doors opened, Meggie forged ahead, leaving him standing alone in the elevator and chuckling.

Her disposition had improved by the time she arrived at the office.

"Morning, Carol." Meggie pulled out the chair to her desk and sat.

"Hi, how did things go last night?" she questioned, rolling her chair back to Meggie's desk and rotating around. "Did you manage to get anything accomplished?"

"Not really," Meggie sighed deeply. "I was interrupted. How about you? Did you have a good time with John?"

Carol's smile was filled with unspoken messages. "Did I ever! We're going out again tonight."

Meggie looked at her friend enviously. Carol and John were so right together, it was obvious they'd probably marry. Why couldn't love and all it entailed be as simple for her? How much easier her life would be if she could have loved Sam and married him. Nothing would have pleased her father more. Yet here she was hundreds of miles from home in love with a man who obviously didn't love her.

By five o'clock, after a busy day, there wasn't much work left on Meggie's desk, but she decided to stay anyway. If she happened to see Quinn he'd think she'd given in to his demands. He had no right to dictate anything to her, least of all her working hours.

At six she had just about completed the one small stack of business that needed her attention. She sat coiled and ready to face Quinn in case he did show.

When she saw his rangy figure moving across the floor toward her, she stiffened resentfully. Forcing herself to concentrate on the policy she was reviewing, she waited for the inevitable confrontation.

"Over here, George."

Unbidden, her heart quickened at the pleasant sound of his rich, low voice. In spite of herself she glanced up to find George carrying a large white sack. Quinn held another.

"This where you want it?" the older man questioned, setting the sack on Carol's desk.

Quinn nodded approvingly. "Great."

"Need anything else?" George's bright smile lit up his dull green eyes.

"Nothing now. Thanks, George."

The old man glanced amusedly at Meggie, then turned and walked away.

Quinn set his sack beside George's on top of Carol's desk.

Finally Meggie could stand it no longer. "Just what are you doing?" she demanded.

"Bringing you dinner," he remarked casually, as if this was the most normal thing in the world. Meggie's eyes widened as he opened a sack and pulled out a candle, placing it on the corner of her desk. He balanced two plates on an uncrowded corner, removing a pile of policies.

"I'm not hungry," she said in an even, quiet voice and could have slapped her stomach for growling at just that moment.

"Pity," Quinn continued. "I'm starved."

As much as she wanted to ignore him, prove her indifference, Meggie couldn't avoid throwing him inquisitive glances as he opened the second bag. Small white boxes with wire handles were ceremoniously placed on the table. Taking Carol's chair, Quinn rolled it around her desk and sat down.

Furiously Meggie closed one policy and reached for another. The aroma of almond chicken hit her with the force of a brick wall. She swallowed back a weakness to succumb; lunch had been hours ago.

"Sure you won't join me?" Quinn asked a moment later.

"I'm sure," she said stubbornly.

"Meggie," he sighed, frustration glinting from his eyes. "You'd sit there and starve rather than eat with me, wouldn't you?"

"That's right," she admitted without looking up from her desk.

"Who would have believed a sweet, little churchgoer could be so stubborn," he mumbled just loud enough for her to hear.

Meggie slammed her pencil down and shot back, "And who would have believed a pillar of the police force could be so rude and behave so chauvinistically."

"Meggie." His voice held a note of warning.

"You have been rotten, Quinn Donnelley," she said, barely holding her quick tongue. "I'm so mad at you I could just scream!"

The muscles at the side of his mouth began to quiver as if he was making an extreme effort not to smile. "Would it do any good if I apologized? If I admitted I behaved high-handedly last night, and asked you politely to join me for dinner?"

Meggie cocked her head to one side and

shrugged her shoulders lightly. "I suppose it might help."

His eyes holding hers captive, Quinn spoke. "There's an awful lot of food here for one person. Would you care to join me, Miss O'Halloran?"

Accepting his hand, Meggie smiled. "Who could ask for a more romantic invitation?"

In gentlemanly fashion, he handed her a plate.

"I should probably have put up more of an argument but I have a terrible weakness for Chinese food."

Quinn cleared his throat, giving the impression of deep shock. "You mean to say it's not my company that interests you, but my choice of cuisine?"

"Absolutely," she told him, dumping a large portion of fried rice onto the plate.

Quinn was quiet for so long that Meggie glanced up to find him studying her. Their eyes locked and she felt like a drowning person. Breathing in deeply, she attempted to regain her composure.

"You've done such a magnificent job. There's only one thing missing," she teased. "Music." The trembling lips were a poor imitation of a smile.

Quinn shook his head slightly. "You have music, don't you?" When she nodded and pointed to a centrally located volume-control switch, he stood and turned the dial. Immediately a soft melody filled the room with the glorious sound of music that seemed to encompass Meggie. Half the time she hardly noticed the music, but with Quinn, now it was the most beautiful sound in all the world. Unconsciously the upper portion of her body began to sway gently with the beat.

"You're a marvel," she said. The romantic mood he had created was an experience she would never forget. "It makes me want to dance."

Quinn glanced around him, making a sweeping study of the empty room, then shrugged lightly. "Why not? Shall we?" He rolled back his chair and stood, offering Meggie his hand.

The smoldering light in his eyes took away her breath and the ready smile faded from his lips as she fitted herself into his arms. With her high-heeled shoes she was nearly as tall as he was. Her arms slid over his shoulders, locking around his neck, while his hands gripped her waist, bringing her boldly against him. He was so close, she could breathe in the masculine scent of his after-shave. Just being in his arms sent shivers of excitement over her skin.

They hadn't moved, each captured in the magic of simply being in one another's embrace. When Quinn began to sway, Meggie followed his lead, gently laying her head on his shoulder. Slowly, ever so slowly, she closed her eyes. The gentle pressure of his mouth against the top of her head stirred the soft auburn curls.

A hand below her chin lifted her face, her name a disturbed throbbing sound as his mouth openly sought hers. Desire seared through her veins as her lips parted voluntarily, eager for the possessive, hungry demand. The kiss that followed was deeper, more intense, as if he couldn't get enough of her, as if he never wanted to let her go.

Shuddering a sigh of longing, Quinn buried his face in her neck, exploring the hollow of her throat and the pulsing cord in the slim column.

The clatter of shoes against the polished floor shattered the heavenly rapture. Shielding her protectively from the gaze of the intruder, Quinn tensed, immediately alert.

"George?" he asked, his voice level, belying the raging fire that had flared between them only a few minutes before. Meggie felt incapable of speech, her lungs robbed of oxygen.

Although George was behind her, Meggie could almost see the older man fluster as he spoke. "Oh, sorry, Donnelley. I was just checking to see if you needed anything . . . and I can see that you . . . well, that you don't."

"Good night, then," Quinn said pointedly, with a heavy note of censure.

"Yes, sir, good night." The chagrined voice faded as if he was walking away as he spoke.

Quinn hesitated momentarily before setting Meggie away from him. The dark eyes were sharp while hers remained soft, drugged by the pleasure his kisses had given her. Meggie marveled at his control.

"You've hardly eaten anything," he reminded her.

Reluctantly, Meggie glanced down at her nearly full plate. "No, I guess I haven't," she murmured.

Holding out her chair, Quinn held it for her as she sat. He paused behind her, his hands resting on the gentle slope of her shoulders before sliding down her arms. His lips teased her neck as she exhaled unevenly.

"Have I told you that you're one of the most beautiful women I've ever known?"

Meggie smiled softly, the corners of her mouth gently curving upward. "And I'd say that one of your ancestors was found kissing the Blarney Stone, Quinn Donnelley," she said, her voice slightly breathless, even now.

Quinn was chuckling to himself as he walked around to the other side of her desk. She met his gaze as he rolled out the chair and sat. With an alluring sweep of her long lashes, she lowered her eyes and concentrated on the meal.

They were silent for a long while, each pretending preoccupation with the dinner. Meggie hardly knew how she managed to maneuver the fork from the plate to her mouth, her thoughts focused on the man sitting across from her. The man she loved. More and more Meggie discovered that her thoughts centered around Quinn, not only when they were together but when they were apart, leading separate lives. She saw so much of herself in Jill and had already come to love the young girl. A longing deep inside prayed that someday the three of them would be a family.

The thought of another child, Quinn's baby, brought an unexpected lump of joy to her throat. A miniature of his father with the same determined jaw and a head full of auburn curls that resembled her hair color. A grandchild was just the healing balm her father needed to smooth him over these difficult years before his retirement and the days he saw his business taken over by Sam or a stranger.

"Are you ready?" Quinn's words splintered the workings of her imagination.

Meggie nodded, helping Quinn load the leftovers into the sacks.

"You look a million miles away," he said, his eyes crinkling with laugh lines. "It must be the company you keep."

"No . . ." She hurriedly discounted the statement until she recognized the twinkle in his eyes.

"Come on, I'll walk you to your car."

The stars glowed like rare jewels against a bed of black velvet. It was a night for lovers. The thought made her sharply aware of the man walking beside her. It was easy to picture Quinn as her lover. He would be gentle, coaxing, patient. His touch, his caresses brought sensations alive within her she hardly knew existed. There was something about Quinn that made her feel more of a woman than any other male. Curiously she wondered what would happen if Quinn could read her thoughts.

"What's so amusing?" he questioned.

Meggie started. "Oh, nothing," she lied.

One thick brow arched challengingly. "If you say so."

At the apartment parking lot, Quinn pulled his Jeep alongside of her Mustang and walked with her to the elevator.

The heavy doors slid shut and Quinn held open his arms in silent invitation. Meggie walked into his embrace, allowing her head to rest upon the muscular chest while his arm curved possessively around her shoulder, cupping her upper arm.

"Any phone calls lately?" he asked in a husky murmur as if he needed something to keep his attention from the fact she was in his arms.

"Hardly ever, anymore. I don't want a tracer on my phone, Quinn. I think whoever was making the calls got bored with me."

"When was the last time he phoned?"

"The Sunday I talked to you," Meggie answered.

Quinn nodded, his expression momentarily hardening. "You realize I unplugged your phone while you were sick, don't you?"

Meggie stared across the blank space of the enclosure. "Yes, I talked to my dad yesterday. He tried to phone last week and was worried when he couldn't reach me." When they'd spoken the night before, Meggie learned it had been Sam who'd made repeated attempts to reach her. Overcome with concern, he'd contacted the phone company and finally informed her father. But how could Meggie be upset with Quinn? He had only been thinking of her.

"I question the fact the caller has lost interest in you, or this game of his," Quinn warned, his eyes narrowed thoughtfully. "Usually when someone has continued for this length of time there's a definite purpose. If you don't want me to place a trace on the line then I think it might be a good idea to get a telephone answering machine."

A short laugh slipped from the tensing muscles of her throat. "I have plenty of other uses for fifty dollars, Quinn." She fixed her gaze on his mouth and felt her heartbeat quicken.

It looked as if he was about to argue when the elevator door glided open. He followed Meggie to her door.

"You're not working overtime tomorrow, are you?"

Leaning against the wall outside her apartment, Meggie's fingers outlined the passionate mouth, trailing over the lean angles of his jaw, her fingertips exploring the muscles as they tightened.

"Meggie," he groaned.

"No, I'm not working overtime," she said with a

seductive smile. "But I'm tempted to know to what lengths you'd travel to keep me from working. I'm mostly caught up now."

His hands bordered the wall on both sides of her face. "You're a stubborn colleen, Meggie O'Halloran," he murmured just before his mouth settled firmly over hers.

The fierce intensity of his touch was gone now. Instead a series of slow, drugging kisses left her breathless and giddy.

Slow to recover from his touch, Meggie was grateful for the wall's support as she leaned her head back, her eyes closed.

"I'll see you in the morning," Quinn whispered, his breathing no less unsteady than hers.

Numbly she nodded.

As it happened, Meggie didn't meet Quinn at the elevator as was their habit the following morning. She waited around for several minutes but then was forced to leave or be late for work.

Quinn was heavy on her mind all day. Would she ever understand this man? He was like two men warring within himself. His sense of God and His love seemed to be as deep and profound as hers. Quinn had shared that part of himself the afternoon he'd taken her to the Grotto. And yet he'd told her not to fill Jill's head with her "phony religion."

Just as confusing were his reactions to her. There could be no doubting his feeling for her ran deep and sure. The way he cared for her while she was ill, and the romantic dinner he'd created last night. The tenderness of his kisses, the barely restrained passion.

Glancing up from her desk, Meggie's brows furrowed with confused uncertainty. It was almost as if Quinn was afraid to love. And not only her; Meggie sensed his doubts were the same toward his daughter. He seemed to be purposely holding himself back from them both. Sometimes when they were together, Meggie could almost visualize a protective shield he erected against her, blotting out her love. He was a man who exuded confidence, a rigid control of his emotions. But Meggie also saw him as a confused, bewildered man.

The days were staying lighter longer now and Meggie changed into comfortable jeans and a sweater for her nightly jaunt. She'd abandoned running; it had become boring and required more energy than she was willing to exert after a full day at the office. Walking seemed to fill the sense of "doing something physical" and she enjoyed the friends she'd made along her nightly route.

There was a friendly collie who met her at his property line and barked loudly to ward her off and at the same time wagged his tail in welcome. Meggie stopped regularly to pet his thick mane. But no matter how familiar she became to him, the dog would always bark at her once. Another dog a couple of blocks from the collie trotted alongside of her, escorting her to the street. Meggie felt the owner must be a jogger because the dog kept perfect time with her brisk pace.

But Meggie's favorite friend was an old man who sat looking out his window and waved at her as she passed. The wave was always accompanied by a bright smile and Meggie felt that the man was housebound, and took great pleasure looking out his window and waving to the passersby.

Setting her pace, Meggie rounded the corner without recognizing the driver of the four-wheel-drive vehicle that eased its way along the curb, following her. The horn caught her off guard and she jumped, startled.

"Quinn!" she admonished, hands resting challengingly on her hips. "You frightened me out of two years' growth."

He was leaning across the seat of the car, speaking through the open passenger window. His lazy smile tripped her already accelerated heartbeat. "You'll have to forgive me for that," he returned evenly. "Now tell me what you're up to, woman."

She gave him a look of total innocence and couldn't help batting her eyelashes. "Nothing but a walk in the fresh air. Come on, join me." She motioned to him with her hand. "The exercise will do you good."

He hesitated just a short moment before pulling

into a vacant space and parking the Jeep. He locked both doors and joined her on the sidewalk, mumbling something imperceptible under his breath.

Tucking her hand inside his elbow, his large hand dwarfed her small one.

"If I may be so bold, may I ask just exactly where you're taking me?" he asked drily.

Meggie's gaze moved thoughtfully over the rugged features. "Oh, about two miles up yonder, maybe less. I keep meaning to gauge it with my car." She smiled. Quinn looked weary, run down. "You don't look so terrific, are you okay?"

"I'm fine," he snapped, a resolute hardness closing over his features.

Meggie stiffened, pulling her hand free. "Sorry I asked," she returned flippantly. She half expected him to apologize, but no regrets followed.

They walked for a couple of blocks, side by side without speaking a word.

"I missed Jill last weekend, where was she?" Meggie asked after a while, hoping to put things back onto an even keel.

"With her grandmother," Quinn stated flatly. "I was busy and didn't want her pestering you."

"Jill doesn't bother me. I enjoy having her around."

"I don't," he spoke with complete calm, matter-of-factly, without rancor.

Meggie glanced at him, unable to disguise her

160

shock. "How can you say that?" she questioned in a small voice. "She's your daughter."

"Don't involve yourself in matters that don't concern you, understand?" The unflinching hardness of his tone brought a lump to Meggie's throat. "Can't we enjoy one another's company without bringing Jill into the conversation? She'll be over this weekend and you can see as much of her as you like. She can spend the whole weekend with you for all I care."

The knot in her throat now gripped her stomach, twisting the sensitive muscles of her abdomen into a painful lump. "For all you care, that child loves you, Quinn. Can't you see that? More important, can't you see what your attitude is doing to her?" she asked, inhaling a wobbly breath.

"I asked you to stay out of my affairs, Meggie," he repeated in a steely voice that brooked no questioning.

Meggie stopped walking, her brow wrinkling with confusion. "I knew from the moment I met Jill that the girl had problems," she said softly. "But I didn't know that you represented ninety percent of what's wrong."

The dark eyes flashed back angrily, his mouth narrowing into a cruel line. "Drop it, Meggie. Jill isn't any concern of yours."

Meggie's mouth opened incredulously. She either had to turn and leave him or let loose with a tongue-lashing that could possibly ruin their relationship. Wordlessly she turned, her mouth pinched tightly shut. She left him standing on the sidewalk, grateful that he didn't attempt to call her back.

Jill was in the hallway outside her apartment when Meggie arrived home Friday afternoon.

"Hi, Jill," she greeted warmly, genuinely pleased to see the girl. "I missed you last weekend."

"I missed you, too," Jill said without meeting Meggie's eyes.

"Is everything all right?"

"Fine," the girl responded quickly, too quickly.

Meggie regarded her doubtfully. "Want to come inside and share a Coke?"

Jill shook her head, her eyes seeming to study Meggie's new shoes.

"Are you sure everything's okay?" It was difficult to disguise the concern in her voice. Jill had never been a very good actress and whatever was bothering her now was all but bursting from unwilling lips.

"I can't stay," she said, her eyes sad. "I've got to get back to the apartment. I'll see you later, okay?"

Meggie watched the curt movements as Jill hurried down the hall to Quinn's apartment. Confused, she shook her head and shrugged lightly before inserting her key into the lock.

There wasn't much Meggie could do for Jill, at least not with Quinn's present attitude.

The fish and chips were browning nicely in the oven when Meggie heard a timid knock on her front door. Jerking her attention from the kitchen, she turned off the oven and pulled the thick mitt from her hand as she crossed the living room.

"Who is it?" she questioned before unlocking the door.

The small voice was trembling. "Jill."

Hurriedly, Meggie opened the door. Tears were streaming down Jill's pale face and she was sobbing almost uncontrollably.

"He made me lie," she cried. "I've been trying so hard to tell the truth and Dad made me lie."

"Jill," Meggie implored urgently. "What is it?"

"I wanted to tell you, but Dad wouldn't let me."

"Tell me what?" Meggie demanded, losing patience.

"Everything's not okay, Meggie. It's Dad. He's real sick, but he told me I couldn't tell you. But he's worse and I don't know what to do."

Chapter Eight

How do you feel?" Meggie questioned, her hand sweeping the damp hair from his brow.

"Rotten," Quinn said and winced.

The memory of speaking with an infected throat was all too recent in Meggie's mind. "Go away," he growled, waving a limp hand dismissively. "I just want to be left alone."

Unable to suppress a smile, Meggie gave an exaggerated curtsey, dipping her head in a subservient manner. "Yes, Your Most Gracious Highness. As you command."

"Meggie." The low growl contained a thin edge of exasperation.

"Okay, I'm going. Want me to close the door on my way out?"

He nodded curtly and Meggie gently eased the door shut. Jill was waiting for her and glanced up expectantly when Meggie entered the room.

"He's better today," Meggie told the girl.

"I did the right thing, didn't I?" Jill's eyes were blue and unsure, and contained a silent plea.

Placing an arm around Jill's shoulder, Meggie reassured her. "I don't know that your father will agree for a while, but I'm glad you came to me, Jill. I'm sure Quinn might have delayed going to the doctor if we hadn't prodded him."

"Will he be all right?"

"Not for a couple of days." Her gaze took note of the strange, brooding quality in Jill's eyes. "But there's nothing to worry about, not when he's on antibiotics."

"Dad's got the same thing you had, doesn't he?" Jill questioned as she sat down on the davenport.

An uneasy sensation came over Meggie. Carefully she watched Jill's expression, realizing the girl could very well be jealous of Meggie's relationship with Quinn.

Jill's mouth tightened. "I bet Dad got sick because he was kissing you." The inflection in her voice made it a question.

Meggie sat beside Jill on the blue velvet couch. "I won't deny that your father has kissed me, if that's what you're asking."

Shrugging her shoulder indifferently as if to show she wasn't really interested, Jill looked away. "Dad likes you, doesn't he?" She vaulted from the sitting position and sauntered into the kitchen before Meggie could respond. Swiveling sharply, she turned back. "Doesn't he?"

All too conscious of the dangerous territory she was entering, Meggie hesitated for an instant. "I hope so, because I like him very much."

"Do you love him?"

The girl had never hesitated to pull any punches, Meggie mused. "Yes," she replied in a steady, unflinching voice, then answered the next question before Jill had the chance to ask it. "I don't know exactly how your father feels about me, but I believe he may love me too."

Jill seemed to appreciate the honesty. "I hope he does," she said in a nearly inaudible voice, slowly shaking her head. Turning around she entered the kitchen. As if the thought had suddenly occurred to her, she jerked herself around, her eyes glinting. "If Dad and you get married, would I come and live with you? We could be a real family."

Meggie exhaled a shuddering breath, gesturing weakly with the open palms of her hands. How had she allowed herself to be trapped into discussing something of such a deep, personal nature, especially when so little was clear between herself and Quinn? "The relationship between your father and me hasn't gone that far. We've never discussed anything resembling a permanent relationship." Meggie stood, hoping to give greater emphasis to her words. "Jill, it would be extremely embarrassing to me if you were to ever repeat what we've just discussed with your father . . . or anyone else, for that matter."

Jill acknowledged her words with a casual dip of her head. "I'm hungry," she announced, her stomach obviously taking priority over the subject matter.

Meggie sighed gratefully and stepped into the kitchen that was a replica of her own, except that everything was situated exactly on the opposite side of the wall from the way it was in her apartment.

Opening the refrigerator, Jill looked inside and wrinkled her nose at an offensive odor. "Yuck, what's that?"

Standing behind Jill, Meggie peered inside and shook her head. "I don't know, but it's certainly colorful, isn't it?" Two timid fingers extracted the container from the barren shelf. Green mold was growing up its edges. "It's taken on a life of its own, whatever it is," she joked, and plugged her nose.

Jill giggled. "Sometimes you can be real funny, Meggie," she said as Meggie gingerly emptied the contents into the sink, turned on the faucet and flipped the wall switch for the garbage disposal.

Opening the freezer section, Meggie eye's grew round with surprise. The entire compartment was stacked with TV dinners of every imaginable size and choice.

"Dad hardly ever cooks," Jill stated in a tired voice. "I'm hungry, but I'm not going to eat that junk again. I'm sick of eating out of cardboard boxes."

"Then it looks like it's up to you to fix something," Meggie said.

"Me?" Jill gasped. "The best I can do is scrambled eggs."

"Good ones, too," Meggie returned softly,

remembering the night Jill had seen to her dinner while Meggie was ill. "Eggs aren't bad, but you need a larger menu, my dear. I think I've got some bacon in my fridge. Maybe we can griddle a few cakes."

Jill's eyes lit up eagerly. "All right, or as my friend, Clare, would say," she paused to laugh, flinging a long strand of hair over her shoulder, "totally tubular."

Even Meggie had to admit that Jill was becoming an accomplished cook. Cleaning up afterwards was a chore both girls enjoyed, laughing and teasing one another as they washed and dried the breakfast dishes.

Glancing questioningly at her wrist watch, Meggie was amazed at the time. "I've got to hurry or be late for church." Whirling around, she stopped, pausing to think. "It is Sunday, isn't it?" The whole weekend had been jumbled in her mind. When Jill had come to tell her about Quinn on Friday afternoon, Meggie had rushed to their apartment. When she'd come in the front door, she had heard Quinn shouting for Jill from one of the bedrooms.

"Jill, where on earth did you go? And it better not be Meggie's," the gruff voice threatened.

Pausing just inside the door, Meggie caught a glimpse of Jill's worried expression.

"Jill," the voice demanded irritably. "Where is that girl?" The words were followed by the sound of impatient movements as if Quinn was shifting about the bedroom.

"Don't worry," Meggie assured Jill quietly. "Let beauty handle the beast."

Jill giggled and then, realizing her father had heard her laughter, clapped a hand over her mouth.

"Jill?" The name was issued in a threatening tone.

"I'm here, too," Meggie called with a slight quiver to her voice.

The list of angry words that followed caused her to wince. More than a little uneasy, Meggie moved into the living room. "Quinn, what's wrong?"

He appeared from the hallway leading off the bedroom. His hair was a mass of tawny confusion; the hastily donned robe was belted at the waist, the deep brown color in sharp contrast to the pale, haggard face.

A frown of concern wrinkled her brow. "Quinn." Involuntarily, his name had slipped from her lips. His mouth tightened into a ruthlessly drawn line. "Who invited you here?" he asked her coldly. Running his fingers through the tangled hair, he glared at her from across the room. "Never mind, I know how you got here. I'll deal with you, Jill, later."

The young girl's chin quivered and Meggie placed a protective arm across her shoulder.

Although it had specifically been against Quinn's wishes, Jill had done the right thing by coming to get her.

"Is it your throat?" Meggie questioned, noting the thin layer of perspiration that beaded his brow.

With a short shake of his head, he slumped against the wall and closed his eyes. "I feel awful."

"You can't feel any worse than you look," she said without censure. "Won't you let me help?"

The tired eyes opened just enough for her to see the pride glinting through. A muscle flexed in the determined jaw. He wouldn't openly admit that he needed her, not when she doubted that he'd even admitted it to himself.

"It's my turn to play nursemaid," she said and released a breath she'd unconsciously been holding. The emotion he was able to arouse within her nearly blocked her mind from clear thinking. Never had there been a time in her life when she wanted to be with anyone more than she did this man right now. "I guess I feel responsible," she added. "I mean, it's probably my fault."

Wearily, Quinn watched her, his mouth tight with an impatient anger.

"Dad," Jill pleaded, confused. "I didn't know what to do. You're so sick. Meggie can help you, I know she can." There was a desperation in the controlled voice that couldn't help but affect Quinn.

As if admitting defeat, he hung his head and gave a short nod. His mouth was quirked in a cynical smile. "But don't imagine that I'm going to let you fawn over me. Get me an aspirin and go mumble a few prayers for me if it'll make you feel any better."

Meggie inhaled a sharp breath; his words seemed to reach out and hit her physically. It was almost as if he purposely wanted to hurt her. Unbidden, tears welled in her eyes, brimming over the thick lashes, embarrassing her.

"Meggie," Quinn groaned and rammed his hands into the pockets of the housecoat. "I'm sorry, I didn't mean that."

Not trusting herself to speak, for fear her voice would crack, she nodded. "Jill will show me where you keep the aspirin," she said, keeping her voice low.

For a moment it looked as if Quinn wanted to say more, but he hesitated and after a tense minute, turned and retreated down the hallway.

"Dad keeps all the medicines and stuff in the bathroom," Jill inserted with an eagerness that showed she would do anything to help.

Meggie watched the retreating male figure until he had entered the bedroom. Jill hadn't exaggerated Quinn's condition and as the evening wore on Meggie became more and more concerned. After the first time Quinn wouldn't allow her to take his temperature again. It had been almost 101 degrees then and if anything, he looked hotter and more uncomfortable now.

Quinn had been vocal about not wanting either of them around; he simply preferred to be left alone. A doctor's appointment had been scheduled for the morning at a Saturday clinic and there was nothing to do but wait out the long night.

Because Jill remained anxious, Meggie spent the night at Quinn's. She'd let him assume she'd returned to her own apartment. If he'd known, she was sure his disapproval would have been vocal and heated. At Jill's insistence she slept in the girl's room, while Jill slept on the sofa.

Restless and concerned about Quinn herself, Meggie couldn't sleep. A clock from the living room chimed the hours as she lay in the dark room. A thin wall was all that separated her from Quinn. If she lay completely still, she was sure she could hear his breathing. The thought was ridiculous, but somehow it comforted Meggie.

About two o'clock, she got up to use the bathroom. A quick check showed that Jill was sleeping soundly, arms and legs flung over the sofa, her blonde head supported by two pillows that were propped against the armrest.

Quinn's door was slightly ajar and Meggie hesitated before entering. The need to assure herself he was resting comfortably overcame caution. Silently she slipped inside his room.

Moon shadows from the open drapes danced

172

across the walls, almost like scenes from a silent movie. The sleeping figure in the bed lay motionless, completely still. Meggie's heart came to her throat at the surge of love she felt for this man. On the opposite side of the room was a desk and chair. She pulled out the chair and sat, watching him, yearning to reach out to touch him, comfort him, love him. Emotions she barely knew existed bubbled to the surface of her being. Never had she felt more a woman, with a woman's emotions, than she did at this moment.

Meggie didn't know how long she sat there watching him sleep. Gradually the dictates of her body took control and her eyelids lowered bit by bit until she fell asleep, slouched in the chair.

"Meggie." Her name was whispered in a coarse, uneven voice.

Flexing the muscles of one shoulder and then the other out of the cramped position, she straightened, her eyes meeting Quinn's.

"What are you doing here?" he questioned gruffly in the same hoarse whisper.

Meggie smiled uncomfortably, her eyes avoiding his. A limp hand swung out, a finger pointing toward the room beside his. "I decided to stay overnight. Jill was worried and I knew I'd be up half the time wondering about you myself, so here I am." She ended in a weak voice.

"You'd probably be a whole lot more comfortable sleeping in Jill's bed, or in your own for that matter." He regarded her sharply, his gaze narrowing. Pausing, he wearily rubbed a hand across his face. "This is crazy," he said, his tone softening. "You're going to make yourself sick again, over me. It's stupid."

The look of tender concern in his eyes created the most wonderful disturbance inside her. "I imagine I'm feeling very much the way you did when I was sick. I need to be here for my own peace of mind. Don't deny me that, Quinn."

He held his hand out to her. Meggie rose, her knees weak under her, but she wasn't sure it was the position she'd fallen asleep in, or the look he was giving her. Taking his hand between her own, she hugged it to her breast and slumped to the floor beside the bed.

"Seeing you there when I woke did something to me," he admitted grudgingly.

Meggie nodded, remembering how she felt the night she'd been so ill and woke to discover Quinn was in the bedroom with her. It had been the night she realized the depth of her love for him.

Tenderly she brought his hand to her mouth and very gently kissed the roughened knuckles. His hand opened, exploring her cheek. An encompassing warmth spread over her.

"Oh, Meggie," he groaned, "it's times like these that I can't think of anything but the feel of you in my arms." His voice was husky in the darkness.

Entwining his fingers in her hair he gently massaged the side of her neck. "When I first saw you, I was sure you were awake. I waited for you to notice me, then I thought you must be praying. There was such a look of total peace about you. I'm sorry for what I said earlier about your praying. I was in pain and I lashed out at you and Jill."

With all the love in her heart shining from her eyes she met his gaze. "It doesn't matter."

"It does matter. Your faith is very much a part of you and I was wrong to have made a joke of your belief in the power of prayer." He dismissed her easy acceptance of his apology. The look of intensity narrowed the dark eyes. "You did pray for me, didn't you, Meggie?"

She nodded, taking his hand between hers again. She leaned forward, their faces almost touching in the small space that separated them. He was lying on the bed, she sitting on the floor, her legs tucked beneath her under the long nylon gown.

"I've wondered how people pray," he said with an absent look. "I know prayer is simply talking to God, but it seems such a waste of valuable time. There's never been anything important enough for me to want to pray about."

"I think you view a man praying as a sign of weakness," she interrupted. "Prayer is a sign of strength. I know that's hard to understand. But I believe you've prayed; you just weren't aware that was what you were doing."

"Meggie." An underlying thread of amusement laced his words. "If I'd prayed, don't you think I'd know it?"

Lowering her eyes, she swallowed at the tightness building in her throat. How could they be so close to one another, not just the physical proximity, but an inner communication that existed between them almost from the beginning? Yet at the same time they were light-years apart. There would have to be a point in his life when he recognized the need to pray, his need for God.

Not long after their talk, Quinn fell into a restless slumber, his hand continuing to hold hers. Eventually the hold slackened and Meggie slipped her slim fingers from his grip. For several minutes afterwards she sat with him, silently picturing Christ's love surrounding them both. A prayer rose automatically to her lips and she murmured it with all the intensity of her love for the sleeping man.

Just as she was about to drop off, Quinn stirred and Meggie shook herself awake. Sore muscles and tired joints would remind her she'd spent the night on a wooden chair and a hard floor if she didn't move. Reluctantly she returned to Jill's bedroom and fell almost immediately into a comfortable and deep sleep.

"Yes, it's Sunday. Do you think I could go to church with you?" Jill's voice interrupted Meggie's thoughts, forcing her into the present. "I have a Bible now," the girl added quickly. "Hariette gave it to me. It's really nice. Want to see?"

"Sure," Meggie nodded, but her attention was riveted on the figure emerging from the hallway.

"What's this about church?" Quinn questioned, his voice tight with impatience, heavy with the connotation that Meggie was going against his wishes for Jill by deliberately inviting her to church.

"I thought you were asleep, Dad," Jill inserted. "I didn't think you'd miss me, but if you're up I'll stay and take care of you while Meggie goes. I don't mind."

Quinn ignored his daughter; instead, his attention rested heavily on Meggie. "I thought we had an understanding?" he questioned with a challenging lift of an arched brow.

Jill glanced anxiously from one to the other. "Remember when we went out to dinner with Meggie, Dad? You said that you thought it might be a good idea if I started attending Sunday school and I said church was a crazy place." Jill laughed. "Since Meggie and I had our talk, I've made some new friends at school. They both attend church. I thought I might like to go sometime. I mean, it can't hurt me, can it?"

"I suppose not," he replied stiffly. "Go ahead and go, the both of you. I could use some peace and quiet for once."

"I didn't realize you found my presence so objectionable," Meggie returned flippantly. "Come on, Jill." She made a hurried movement for the door.

"Meggie," the gruff voice stopped her. She tensed as she turned toward him. His dark eyes staring back at her were unfathomable pools she would never understand. "Jill's grandmother is coming by about twelve-thirty to pick her up. Will you be back by then?"

"I'll make a point of it," she said with a straight back, her eyes glinting with barely restrained aggression. He seemed surprised at the angry flecks in her dark eyes. To her chagrin, her irritation seemed to amuse him and he tried, unsuccessfully, to contain a smile.

"I don't see what you find so all-fired funny, Quinn Donnelley," she murmured between clenched teeth.

"Maybe I should change my clothes," Jill interrupted, obviously unaware of the surly undertones passing between her father and Meggie.

"Go ahead," Quinn said without looking at Jill.

"You look fine just the way you are," Meggie contradicted.

"Better not change if there isn't time," Quinn advised. "There's nothing worse than a church full of people watching you make a grand entrance because you're late. And Meggie," he continued, "your Irish ancestry is showing again."

Her brown eyes rounded incredulously. He had purposely riled her and then stood there, silently laughing, when she reacted to his anger.

Meggie and Jill were back on the stroke of twelve-thirty. Hariette was sitting in her car outside the apartment building when they pulled into the parking lot.

"Tell Dad I left with Hariette, okay?" Jill said as she leaped out the door.

"Jill, wait," Meggie insisted. For the present she wanted to avoid Quinn as much as possible, at least give him the time to recuperate without someone fussing over him. He didn't want her there and would assume she'd made an excuse to see him if she delivered the message.

"Why?" Jill asked impatiently. "Hariette's waiting!"

"Don't you need to get your things first?" she asked on a hopeful note.

"No, I thought I told you, I keep a lot of my things at Dad's. It's a hassle taking things back and forth every weekend."

"All right," Meggie said with a weak smile and sighed. "I'll see you next Friday." With a quick wave of her hand, Jill ran to meet her grandmother.

Rather than personally deliver Jill's message, Meggie decided to phone.

"Yes." Quinn's response was made in a gruff, unfriendly voice.

"It's Meggie," she returned quickly. "Hariette met us outside the building. Jill wanted me to let you know that she's gone with her grandmother. I apologize if I disturbed your solitude," she said in a voice that was dipped in honey. She could hear his soft chuckle as she replaced the phone receiver.

Several times during the remainder of the afternoon Meggie had to force herself not to make an excuse to visit Quinn. Again and again she found her thoughts centering on him. She was behaving worse than a worried wife. Was he taking the medication the doctor ordered according to directions?

Meggie had brought the tablets in to him with a glass of water before. Maybe he didn't know where she'd placed the prescription? Did he need her to fix him something to eat? He had never invited her into his apartment; if she checked up on him, would he resent the intrusion into his privacy? A hundred questions shot out at her every time she turned around. It was impossible to keep her mind involved in anything. Not a letter to her friend Jacquie, not a phone call to her father, not a classic Hollywood movie playing on the television. Nothing.

Finally, when she was totally disgusted with herself, she took a bath, soaking in the hot, scented water for a long time, to relax her mind as well as her body. The long auburn curls remained piled high on her head as she slipped into a full-length velour robe that zipped up the front. Matching slippers, the same color pink as the robe, covered her feet.

Sorting through the cupboards for an idea of something to fix for dinner, Meggie was surprised at the rapid knock at her front door. A hand replaced a stray curl in a disconcerted movement as she walked across the room.

"Yes," she called.

"It's Quinn," came the muted reply.

Her hands fumbled slightly as Meggie turned the dead-bolt lock, stepping aside to admit him. Crazily she half expected him to vanish as if her imagination had conjured up his image.

"Can I come in?" he questioned.

"Of course," Meggie replied, amazed he had come to her. "Are you feeling all right?" She could have bitten her tongue the minute the words were out. The last thing she wanted was for him to realize how much she was concerned.

"Fine thanks." He sauntered past her, into the living room, to stand in front of the television. "Movie any good?" He looked at her expectantly.

Meggie wasn't aware she'd left the TV on. "I wasn't really watching it," she said; her emotions remained confused and slightly muddled. "I was just going to fix myself some dinner. Would you like something to eat?"

"Sure." He lowered himself onto her couch, his

gaze leaving her to flicker briefly over the TV screen.

Why was it after all these weeks that Quinn had the power to unnerve her? While she was busy in the kitchen using what she could find to mix together an appetizing casserole, Quinn remained in the living room, seemingly engrossed in the movie.

When she could no longer make an excuse to remain in the other room, Meggie moved into the living room with Quinn, positioning herself at the other end of the couch.

Quinn glanced over to her and smiled one of those devastating smiles that had the power to melt her bones, his outstretched arm indicating he wanted her to sit beside him. The thought of not accepting the silent invitation didn't occur to Meggie. There wasn't anyplace in the world she'd rather be than near this man.

Quinn's hand reached over and cupped her shoulder, bringing her against him.

"Why did you come?" she asked, pretending an interest in the movie.

The lines of his mouth deepened into smiling grooves as she glanced at him. "For all my complaints about wanting peace and quiet, I discovered I was lonely without you fussing over me," he admitted with a chagrined edge to his voice. "I like having you around, Meggie, it's something I could become very accustomed to. I didn't know I was coming. I just got dressed and came. I wanted to be with you."

"Oh, Quinn," she said and sighed, nestling closer to him, enjoying the feel of his sweater against her face, the uneven breath that stirred the stray curls at her ear and the gentle feel of his lips as they sought the sensitive cord of her neck. Her pulse hammered in her throat as waves of pleasure swept over her. When she raised her head, she found him staring at her with a disturbing intensity.

Slowly, deliberately, his fingers released each pin from her hair, sending her curls cascading down her shoulders. His fingers slid into the thickness, tilting her head back so her mouth could receive his kiss.

Meggie returned the hunger of his exploring kiss, opening her mouth to him. Pliant and responsive, she lay in his arms, a helpless victim of their love. Throughout her life, Meggie had wondered if she would ever love a man as deeply as she did Quinn. The intensity of her emotions shocked her now. There was no thought of her pride or her defenses; all she felt was a deep and abiding love for this man who was capable of drugging her senses with the touch of his mouth.

"Dinner . . . is ready. . . ." she stammered at the sound of the timer from the stove.

Quinn's hold loosened and he released her with a reluctance that thrilled her all the more.

Meggie stood on legs that threatened not to support her and moved into the kitchen. Opening a drawer, she took out a potholder.

Quinn followed her, sliding both hands around her waist, bringing her back against him, molding her against the length of his masculine frame. Meggie inhaled sharply as he buried his face in the side of her neck, and closed her eyes to the swelling tide of passion he could arouse within her.

"I want you, Meggie," he whispered with a tenderness that took her breath away. "I never wanted anyone the way I want you right now. But more than that, I love you. I didn't mean for that to happen. Loving you caught me unaware. I fought against it," he admitted. "I don't think I realized the depth of my feelings until I woke up the other night when I was sick and found you sleeping in my room. Something happened to me as I watched you. I realized I couldn't live without you, without your love. I needed you."

"Oh, Quinn," she whispered on a long sigh, "I love you too." She turned and her hands slid over the craggy line of his jaw, tenderly cupping his face as she smiled into his eyes. "How I've prayed that you would love me. I don't think I could bear to live without you now."

"You've given me a reason to dream again," he mumbled against her hair.

"I have a dream," she said softly. "If I close my

eyes I can picture our child." Her eyes misted with tears at the tremulously happy picture her mind was forming. "He has your chin, strong and determined; his hair is the same shade of auburn as mine," she added.

"I'd like a son," Quinn said with a wistful timbre in his voice. "I never dared hope that I'd have a family. I'd never believed anyone could come into my life the way you have."

"Oh, Quinn," she murmured through the fog of happiness that surrounded her. She closed her eyes and leaned against him. The lump of joy was building in her throat until it was almost impossible to talk.

His chuckle caused her to open her eyes. "Is 'Oh, Quinn,' all you can say, woman?"

Their gazes met, her eyes brimming with tears, smiling up at him with all the love in her heart.

"We'll build a good life, the three of us."

"The three of us?" There was a questioning quality in his tone.

"Yes, silly. You, Jill and me."

His gaze narrowed, almost angry as he glared at an object behind her. "We'll build a life together, Meggie, but Jill won't be included."

Meggie stared at him in complete bewilderment. "How can you say that?" she asked, incredulous. "Jill's your daughter, your own flesh and blood. I love her, she's part of you."

Pulling her arms loose from around his waist,

185

Quinn turned and ran a hand over his tired features. "Don't misunderstand me, I'm pleased you love Jill. She needs that. But she won't be a part of you and me. She'd ruin our love, destroy what's between us."

"Quinn," Meggie pleaded. "You're not making any sense. How could Jill possibly destroy our love?"

The doorbell chimed, catching Meggie off guard. She glanced toward the living room, her brow knit questioningly. She wasn't expecting anyone.

Quinn rammed his hands into his pockets and just as forcibly jerked them out again and raked his fingers through his hair. "There's something you need to understand, Meggie," he said crisply, with a piercing look that cut right into her. "I never wanted Jill."

The doorbell chimed again this time, with two short, impatient rings.

"But Jill's your daughter," Meggie murmured fervently, walking across the apartment. She was turning the lock but paused before opening the door when Quinn spoke again.

"Not only did I never want Jill, I've never loved her because . . ." He stopped abruptly, the color draining from his face as Meggie opened the door.

Framed in the doorway, her eyes incredulously round and full of such pain that Meggie had to stifle a cry of alarm, was Jill.

Chapter Nine

W hat's the matter, pumpkin? You don't sound right. Is it Quinn?" Meggie's father asked, in a gentle, assuring tone.

Meggie felt tears beginning to sting the back of her eyes. "Yes," she said in a weak voice that was barely audible over the telephone line. "Everything's such a mess between us. I don't know that it will ever be the same again."

"I wouldn't worry if I were you, Meggie. If it was meant to be then things will work out right."

Her father's psychological approach didn't comfort her any, but she grudgingly admitted he was right. "I suppose so," she said, her mouth tightening.

"If things don't straighten themselves out you can always come home."

The implication was there that Sam would always be waiting for her, but Meggie chose to ignore the unspoken suggestion.

"No, Dad," she said in a lowered voice. "My home is in Portland now. Whatever happens between Quinn and me has nothing to do with returning home."

A lengthy pause followed. "Whatever you think is best." There was a note of finality in his voice as if he had completely accepted the fact that she would never marry Sam.

Their conversation lasted only a few minutes longer. After replacing the receiver, Meggie sat in her living room, oblivious to all that was happening around her. The whole world could have gone into a tailspin and she wouldn't have noticed or cared. The look of such deep pain in Jill's eyes continued to haunt Meggie. How could Quinn be so insensitive to his daughter? It cut at her heart as sharply and painfully as a knife slicing into her flesh.

Jill did her best to pretend she hadn't heard Quinn, but she didn't fool Meggie. Not for a second.

Quinn had been shocked too and reacted with anger. "What are you doing here?" he'd demanded of Jill.

"I . . . I forgot one of my school books that I need Monday. Hariette drove me back . . . but you were gone and I didn't have my key. I thought Meggie might know where you were. I didn't mean to interrupt anything," she had murmured abjectly.

"You didn't," Meggie had interjected, her dark eyes shifting to Quinn, glittering with anger.

"No, as a matter of fact, you didn't," Quinn had concurred. "I was just leaving, wasn't I Meggie?"

"Yes . . . yes, you were," she'd said. Her trembling fingers had remained clenching the doorknob; she'd opened the door wider, indicating she was ready, more than ready, to have him leave. Without another word he'd walked out of the apartment.

That was the last time Meggie had spoken to Quinn. Three days. Three of the longest days of her life. They met every morning at the elevator, treating each other like polite strangers. Neither speaking, ignoring one another so completely no one would have guessed that only a few days before they had openly declared their love and talked of marriage and children. Meggie didn't know how much longer they could continue like this. It was ridiculous and yet she hadn't the courage to make things any different.

When Jill didn't show up the following weekend, Meggie phoned Hariette and was told that Jill had a bad case of the flu and would probably be fine by next Friday. When subtly questioned, the woman assured Meggie that other than the flu, Jill had behaved in a perfectly normal way during the week. It was only Thursday night that Jill had come down with the flu.

Monday morning, the thick, gray clouds matched the gloom in Meggie's heart. She met Quinn outside the elevator and the silence that stretched between them gnawed at her soul. Wordlessly they stepped inside the vacant doors together. Mechanically Quinn punched the button for the bottom floor for both of them. Meggie concentrated her gaze on the illuminating light that indicated the floor number rather than look at Quinn.

They had begun the descent when suddenly the elevator jerked, everything went dark and a piercing bell began to ring.

With a cry of fright, Meggie covered her ears and instinctively moved to Quinn's side. "What's happening, what's wrong?" she cried urgently.

His arms wrapped around her automatically, pulling her into his protective embrace. "I don't know," he murmured.

The bell stopped and Meggie uncovered her ears.

"It must be a power outage," Quinn said, confirming Meggie's own assessment of the situation.

It was black as pitch inside the tiny cubicle and impossible to see beyond a few feet. Not that it mattered. Meggie wouldn't have moved; she was in Quinn's arms again and no matter what needed to be said between them, no matter what the outcome—it felt so right.

Without self-directing thought, her arms slid around his waist as she laid her head against his chest; his heartbeat hammering evenly against her ear was soothing and comforting.

"If this is what it takes to get you back in my arms then I hope the power never comes back on again," Quinn murmured against her hair. His mouth sought her temple, gently caressing the soft skin at the side of her face.

With a supreme effort of her will, Meggie gave a faint cry and pulled herself free. Her eyes had adjusted to the dark enough to see the weary look come over Quinn. It was crazy. She saw him every day, yet it took one glance in a dark elevator for her to see how troubled he was. Lines pinched his mouth; his eyes were dull and so weary she longed to ease the ache from him. He was slouched forward as if carrying a load heavier than any man was meant to support.

Meggie bit into her bottom lip, tears welling in her eyes. "Oh, Quinn," she mumbled miserably. Tentatively she reached out a hand, gently massaging his face, exploring the lines of his jaw and chin.

A rough hand stopped her, taking her palm to his lips. "Meggie, I love you," he murmured with such tenderness it nearly caused her to weep.

"Oh, Quinn," she managed on a sniffle.

"Here we go with the 'Oh, Quinns' again," he teased.

Meggie attempted to laugh, but the sound was more of a strangled noise that came deep from within her throat. "I've been so miserable without you. We've got to talk, make things right with Jill."

Quinn stiffened against her, gently pushing her

away. "Things are never going to be right between Jill and me," he said in an abrupt, clipped voice. "It's unfortunate if she heard me the other night, but I didn't say anything she doesn't already know."

Meggie stood like a statue, so incredibly shocked she couldn't move, couldn't breathe, could barely think. "I don't believe I'm hearing this," she said in a tightly controlled voice. "What could this child possibly have done for you to dislike her so intensely?"

Quinn was quiet for a long moment. "Jill isn't my daughter."

Meggie's eyes rounded incredulously. "Of course, she's your daughter," she countered. "A hundred times I've seen you in her, the way she says things, the way she looks sometimes, that spark of determination in her eye."

Quinn's returning laugh held little humor. "That isn't my look you see in Jill. It's Nelson Bennett." Quinn's hand reached for hers. "It's a long story and it looks like we might be here for a while." He removed his coat and spread it on the elevator floor. "Let's sit down."

Meggie sat. Quinn placed a hand around her, cradling her in the crook of his arm. He was quiet for so long, she wondered if he'd changed his mind.

"My parents were killed in a car accident when I was nineteen," he began after several minutes. By the way he spoke, Meggie could hear how difficult it was for him to relate the story. "It's an emotional time in anyone's life, but I was fortunate to have known their love. My two younger brothers and little sister went to live with a maiden aunt. I helped out as much as I could but was drafted soon afterwards. While I was in Vietnam and Thailand, Anson and Cal graduated and made lives for themselves. By the time I returned Diana was fifteen. I don't think I've seen a more beautiful fifteen-year-old than Diana. But she lacked guidance in her life, she ran around with the wrong crowd, experimented with drugs until eventually she was hooked. Nelson Bennett was her connection. I met Laura, Jill's mother, through Diana. She was older and had been around. When Laura told me she was pregnant, I didn't doubt I was the father. After we got married I wanted Diana to come and live with us, but Laura was having a difficult time with the pregnancy and didn't want my kid sister around." He paused and Meggie could feel the tension building inside of him. His grip on her tightened as he fought to control his emotion, as if reliving this was more painful than she would ever know. "I had been accepted into the police academy by this time. Having a cop for a brother was a joke to Diana; she openly flaunted her involvement with drugs, knowing I'd never arrest her. If I'd known at the time it was Nelson who was supplying her I would have done anything I could to have stopped him.

"Six months after Laura and I were married Jill was born. In the beginning I may have had some fatherly interest in her, but I doubt it. She was a sickly baby, crying all the time. I don't know that I even held her more than once or twice. She didn't seem any more inclined toward me than I was toward her.

"Jill was only a few months old when Diana overdosed. I was the one who found her, the needle still in her vein." He stopped and Meggie could hear him inhaling deep breaths at the memory. "I didn't rest until I found who'd sold her the drugs. I was like a madman hunting Nelson Bennett down, not sleeping, not eating, working day and night. By the time I found him I'd collected enough evidence to put him away for life. Not long after the trial Laura and I had a big fight and she told me I wasn't Jill's father, Nelson was. Again and again she screamed that I was responsible for Nelson's prison term. In the beginning I wanted to believe she had said it out of some twisted hatred for me, but as time wore on I could see it was the truth. Every time I looked at Jill I saw Nelson. Laura and I separated when Jill was barely a year old. A few years ago, Laura got drunk and smashed a car into a tree, killing herself. I didn't want Jill living with me then; I don't want her now."

"But, Quinn." Meggie was at a loss for words,

struggling to know what to say, where to begin. "Can't you see that Jill is innocent in all this? She of all is blameless. When you look at Jill, you aren't seeing Nelson, you're seeing that unhappiness all over again."

"I told you before that Jill would destroy our love, ruin our chances for happiness. Don't you see that it's happening already?"

Inhaling an uneven breath to steady her nerves, Meggie began again. "No, I don't. All I see is a man tortured by guilt. You feel guilty because you couldn't help your own sister, guilty because Nelson Bennett is spending the remainder of his life rotting in a prison cell. That guilt is in your voice as plain as if you'd spoken the words. It's not Jill, it's the memory."

"It isn't." The refusal came sharp and vigorous. "Who can blame me for wanting to start a new life? I want to leave the past behind me. Can't you understand the impossibility of doing that with Jill?" His voice was raised and forceful, as if he needed the higher volume to make his point.

Slipping her arms around him, Meggie pressed her cheek to the gentle slope of his neck, her tongue tasting the spicy after-shave he had applied that morning. "I love you, Quinn, but I can see that we can't build a future until you've settled the past."

"It's settled," he argued in an unreasonable

voice. "I suppose you're going to tell me that Christ has made everything right and I can go on my merry way. Well, where I come from that's not the way things are handled."

If Quinn was expecting an angry response from Meggie she didn't have one for him. "No, but I will tell you that I know personally what guilt can do to someone. I've lived with it, when I couldn't do what my dad wanted from me. One thing I learned, Quinn. I discovered there's nothing I can do to make Christ love me more, and by the same token, there's nothing I can do to make Him love me less. Until you can accept that, our relationship will be at a standstill."

He was quiet for so long afterwards that Meggie wondered if she'd said too much, gone too far. An intolerable sadness came over her. It was happening again. Only inches separated them physically, yet whole worlds stood between them.

Each minute passed with an interminable slowness as they sat, arms around one another, in the darkened elevator.

"I'm glad you're with me," she whispered after a while. "I'd have been frightened to death in here alone." Meggie could feel the nod of his chin against the top of her head. "I've been receiving the phone calls again, worse than ever. Sometimes two and three times a night."

The grip of his arms tightened. "Why didn't you tell me?"

"I just did," she said and smiled.

"I mean before now. How long has this been going on?"

"It started again the middle of last week."

"Think, Meggie, what happened in your life last week? There's got to be some connection. I'm convinced whoever is making these calls is someone you know and talk to every day." Although there was a soft urgency in his voice, he continued to hold her, his hand stroking her hair as if they were discussing Wall Street and not some demented thrill-seeker.

Mentally she ran through every day of the week, her memory tainted by the confusion between Quinn and herself. Thoughtfully she shook her head. "There's nothing. I went to work every day like always. Had lunch with Carol Saturday afternoon, church on Sunday and then back to the salt mines Monday morning again."

Meggie could hear the frustrated sigh. "Are you sure you don't recognize the voice?"

"I can't," she said, feeling the same frustration. "The voice is muffled. I couldn't recognize my own father the way this guy speaks. I phoned the telephone business office and am having my number changed again, but that isn't any solution. If you'd like you can come over this evening and listen yourself; maybe you can make out something I can't. He usually phones about the same time. It's gotten to the point that I just pick up the phone and replace the receiver every night about eight."

"I couldn't stand it if something happened to you, Meggie," he mumbled into her hair. The softly spoken words, more than anything, showed the depth of his feelings for her.

"Nothing's going to happen to me," she assured him. "In the beginning of all this I was terrified. Then one Sunday I was sitting in church and I had the most peaceful feeling come over me. I don't think there's any way to describe it. But ever since, I've found the calls a nuisance, but they haven't frightened me."

A hint of anger reverberated in his husky voice. "Meggie, you're too intelligent to believe that. I don't want you to worry or make yourself paranoid, but there's got to be something more than this religious comfort."

"There isn't," she began, yearning to explain, yet knowing it was useless. Quinn wouldn't understand.

The elevator made a churning noise and the lights suddenly flashed. It took several minutes to readjust her eyes to the light. Meggie squinted at her watch and noticed they had been trapped in the elevator for over an hour.

Quinn helped her up and retrieved his coat, brushing off the dirt before laying it across his forearm.

The elevator began to move and as they stepped

into the apartment building's foyer, Meggie had the craziest compulsion to stop and murmur a silent "thank you." There was no way of telling how long it would have been before Quinn told her of his past if it hadn't been for the power outage. As it was his hand rested gently against the small of her back, directing her as they walked to the parking lot.

The manager and a couple of others were waiting outside in the foyer when Meggie and Quinn walked off. Meggie was mildly surprised at the amount of interest their little adventure had aroused. But she quickly dismissed the concern. She was already forty minutes late for work and didn't want to waste any more time.

Quinn's Jeep was parked down from her car. He paused as she inserted her key into the door of her Mustang. "I'll see you tonight, Meggie." He leaned forward, his lips brushing hers in a sweet, sensuous kiss that blocked out all conscious awareness but the feel of his mouth over hers.

"Okay," she said and smiled, wishing she had such a kiss to send her off every morning.

For such a shaky beginning Meggie had a good day. She was busy, and although her thoughts were with Quinn they weren't preoccupied as they had been the last few days. Several times during the morning Meggie found herself consciously listening to people's voices, hoping to find some connection with the voice on the phone. It was hopeless. Not only didn't she have a clue as to who would want to frighten her, she found it difficult to suspect anyone.

About noon, just as Meggie was ready to go to lunch, she saw Quinn walking across the floor. Several girls stopped working to watch him. Meggie couldn't blame them. Quinn had the male magnetism that captured a woman's attention. It was amazing really, because he wasn't handsome. Not in the normal sense. Meggie couldn't restrain the stirrings of pride as he stepped to her desk.

"Can I take you to lunch?" His eyes held unspoken messages that were only for her.

"I suppose I could be persuaded." She smiled up at him. Reaching for her purse, she scooted out of the chair and stood.

"Introduce me, Meggie. I'd like to meet the people you work with."

Meggie almost laughed. Quinn wasn't interested in these people; he had come with the object of learning who was in her office in the hopes of tracking down the caller. "Why?" she questioned him bluntly.

His brows arched as he reached for her hand. "As your future husband I'd like to meet your friends."

Just having him say the words did erratic things to Meggie's heartbeat. "You're not fooling me," she said softly, leading him to the department head's office.

"I didn't expect to," he returned just as softly, his eyes smiling deeply into hers.

"Well, did anyone give you the impression they were lunatics in disguise?" Meggie tried to make a joke of it as she pushed the half-eaten salad aside. Quinn had been unusually quiet during lunch. Meggie could almost visualize his mind churning, tabulating details she would probably never have noticed about her coworkers. She had issued an invitation to dinner but he barely seemed to notice or hear her.

"Is it my deodorant or something?" she asked finally, after he'd ignored practically every attempt she'd made toward conversation.

His returning smile held a puzzled twist. "Pardon?"

She batted her eyelashes at him wickedly. "I was asking about dinner," she repeated. He obviously hadn't heard either comment.

He waved his hand across his plate. "No thanks, I just ate."

"Quinn!" She said his name in a low growl. "You're doing this purposely to drive me crazy, aren't you?"

"Doing what?" He looked at her blankly.

Slowly shaking her head, she felt a smile tugging at the corners of her mouth. "Never mind." She sighed. Somehow she knew it would always be like this with Quinn. She supposed she should be offended that her stimulating personality didn't overcome him completely, that he didn't hang on her every word. Instead, she was pleased in a silly sort of way. His acceptance of her into his life was total; he was treating her very much like the wife she would become.

"I thought I'd fix green eggs and ham, how does that sound?"

He lifted the coffee cup to his mouth, downing the contents in one swallow. "Great," he replied absently.

Now, several hours later, Quinn looked down at the plate of spaghetti. "I thought you said something about ham and a ridiculous color of eggs," he questioned, totally serious.

Meggie had just opened the oven door to take out the french bread. She was so surprised that she dropped her potholder and seared two fingers on the rack.

"Darn," she cried, sticking the fingers in her mouth.

Feigned shock rounded his eyes as she turned around to glare at him accusingly. "Such language." He tilted his head with mocking reproval. "If you want to marry a police inspector you must learn to watch your tongue, woman. Want me to kiss it better?" he offered in feigned sympathy.

"Please." She held out her hand.

"It wasn't your fingers I had in mind." His gaze was resting on her softly parted lips.

The intensity of his look was enough to make her knees weak. "Why is it you can tease me and make it sound more beautiful than poetry?"

"Because I love you," he said matter-of-factly.

"Oh, Quinn."

Their eyes met, each holding unspoken promises. "We're going to have to do something with this lack of vocabulary, Mary-Margaret O'Halloran."

The phone rang, and for a second Meggie's heart stopped, her gaze swinging from the kitchen to the oak end table in her living room.

"Do you want me to answer it?" Quinn asked, the teasing banter instantly gone from his voice. There was something so cold and so hard in his tone, it forced her attention from the telephone to him.

"No." She shook her head. "I doubt that it's him. It's not eight yet." The walk across the room seemed as long and as far as her nightly treks around the neighborhood. "Hello." She couldn't avoid the breathless quality to her voice.

Silence. Meggie's eyes sought Quinn; she raised her hand, palm up, to show her confusion.

"Meggie," the small voice came at last. "It's Jill."

"Jill," she repeated the name, both relieved and surprised. "How are you?" She turned around so Quinn couldn't watch her as she spoke.

"Fine," came the same small voice.

"You don't sound right; what's wrong?"

"I got braces today."

For a half-second Meggie had been afraid something had gone terribly wrong and now she couldn't prevent the soft laugh. "Now I know why your voice sounds so timid. It hurts to talk, doesn't it?"

"Yes," Jill murmured, but Meggie could still hear the urgency in her young voice. "Did you have braces when you were my age?"

Meggie groaned at the memory. "Yes, but I was sixteen and I got them on two days before a big school dance. I was afraid to open my mouth. My date thought I was a real nerd."

Jill giggled and Meggie felt a sigh of relief come over her. Her prayers these last few days had centered heavily on the girl. To hear a laugh, however small, boosted Meggie's spirits. "Are you coming Friday afternoon?"

Jill hesitated, her voice uncertain. "That was what I was calling about. I was wondering if it would be all right if I spent the night with you. I mean, Dad's busy so much and I'd . . ." Her thin voice wavered slightly.

"You can spend the night with me any time you like. But I think you'd better get your dad's approval."

"He doesn't care," she returned automatically.

It wasn't just spending the night Jill was

referring to and they both knew it. "I have something for you when you come," Meggie encouraged her enthusiastically. "It's a T-shirt, from the time I was in braces, I want you to have."

"Really? What does it say?"

Meggie smiled at the memory; her father had gotten her the shirt and had it specially printed for her. It was unique, one of a kind. "It says: DOING TIME, BUT GOING STRAIGHT."

Jill giggled again. "I've got to go. I'll see you Friday, okay?"

"Okay," Meggie said softly and replaced the receiver.

When Meggie turned around she noticed Quinn was standing at the sliding glass door, looking out over the city. When he turned toward her his face was twisted in a heavy scowl.

"What's wrong?" Meggie asked.

He rubbed a hand over his face, his eyes dull, defeated. "Jill," he said, "is up to her tricks again."

"What do you mean?"

"She's not getting braces," he finished.

Chapter Ten

M eggie was crying. She didn't know why the tears had filled her eyes, brimming over the rim of thick lashes. One ignominious tear gave way, bursting the whole dam until they fell unrestrained down her pale face.

"Meggie, what is it?" Quinn's threatening frown was replaced by a look of tender concern. He moved away from the glass door until he stood in front of her. Ever so gently his fingers wiped a tear from her face. "It was bound to happen. You must realize that," he said in a low voice that spoke of his own frustration. "Jill is incapable of telling the truth. Hariette and I talked about braces for her last year, but nothing was decided."

"I want to believe her."

"I do too," he added, "but past experience has taught me I can't. Jill's mother was the same way. I soon learned she couldn't be trusted either."

Meggie's hand stopped Quinn's, his face swimming before hers as she spoke. "If you couldn't trust Laura then how can you believe what she told you about Jill?"

Quinn's returning smile was cold. "One look at Jill says Laura was telling the truth." The words were as stiff as the smile that slashed his face. His hand fell limply to his side.

"Quinn," Meggie spoke tentatively. "We've got

to settle this thing with Jill. She's going to need professional help, and lots of love."

"Hariette loves her."

"Yes," Meggie interrupted, "but I've seen Hariette. She's getting old and can't be expected to take care of Jill much longer. A decision must be made sooner or later."

"Meggie," he said and sighed, a finger lifting her chin fractionally so his gaze could skim her face. "I know what you're trying to do, but it isn't going to work. Jill will remain with her grandmother as long as she can. When she can't then I'll make some other arrangements. But I won't have her interrupting our lives. What we have is too precious; I won't chance having our happiness together ruined."

Miserably, Meggie nodded.

If Quinn had been quiet during lunch, it was Meggie who was preoccupied during the evening meal. Twice Quinn attempted to draw her into conversation. Although she answered him, her thoughts were a thousand fathoms deep. Finally Quinn gave up the effort to make conversation.

The phone rang at exactly eight. A restraining hand stopped Meggie as she moved to answer it.

Quinn lifted the receiver and silently placed it to his ear. A hand over her mouth, Meggie watched his guarded expression and the involuntary flicker of revulsion that showed in his eyes. A few minutes later, Quinn replaced the receiver.

"Will he phone again?" he asked, after a moment's pause.

Meggie nodded. "Usually in about an hour."

Quinn breathed in deeply. "Then let's be ready. I think it's time we found out exactly what this guy is after."

Meggie looked up, surprised, her brown eyes rounding with uncertainty. She didn't want to know what the caller wanted, she just wanted to be left alone. "But how?"

Quinn sat, withdrawing a pen and pad from his jacket pocket. "I'll answer if he calls again and listen to what he says. When I give you the signal, I want you to say one of the following responses into the receiver, then give me back the phone." His hand furiously wrote out several phrases. "I'll point to the one I want you to say. Understand?"

Her agreeing nod was nothing more than a nervous tremor.

"I love you, Meggie," he whispered and lowered his head, covering her mouth with his. He kissed her as if she was the most delicate, most precious being in the world. Subtly, his lips parted hers, deepening the contact.

Meggie's arm circled his neck as the radiating warmth spread over her. The kiss grew bolder as his hands found the small of her back, molding her against his lean length. They fit together as if God had created them for one another. Meggie could never doubt that God had given her Quinn.

With a sighing moan, Quinn broke the contact, burying his face in the hollow of her neck. Several seconds passed before he seemed composed enough to speak. "The time is coming when I'm not going to be able to repress the desire to make you completely mine. I want you for my wife and the sooner the better."

"Oh, Quinn," she moaned, running her fingers through his hair, loving the feel of his lips against her flesh.

The soft chuckle made her realize what she'd said and she smiled, shaking her head at her sad lack of anything romantic beyond his name.

The wait for the second call wasn't as long as Meggie had anticipated. The minute the phone sounded, Meggie's eyes flew to Quinn. He smiled reassuringly and, taking her hand to his mouth, he gently brushed his lips over her fingertips. The loving action stilled the frantic beat of her heart.

"I want you to say hello," he instructed, picking up the phone and placing it against her ear.

"Hello," Meggie spoke hesitatingly. At the lash of obscenities, she squeezed her eyes shut.

Immediately Quinn took the phone and placed it against his ear. With his pen he pointed to one of the phrases he had written and gave Meggie back the receiver.

"What do you want?" she demanded, forcing her voice to sound decisive, angry.

Quinn nodded approvingly, taking back the phone.

Several more times, Meggie spoke into the receiver saying things such as: "No, don't say that." "But why?" "I'll do anything, only leave me alone." "Yes. Yes."

Although it seemed an eternity, it was only a few minutes later when Quinn replaced the receiver in its cradle. "Well?" Meggie questioned with anxious eyes. "What did he say?"

As if still absorbing the conversation, Quinn responded with an abrupt shake of his head. "Plenty," he murmured thoughtfully.

"Enough for you to get a clue as to who it might be?"

He didn't answer for a moment, his eyes drinking deeply from hers. "Yes," he said as he placed a hand at the back of her neck and directed her mouth to his. With barely restrained urgency his mouth covered hers, hardening with the intensity of his ardor. Quinn's lovemaking had always been gentle; now the harsh possession of his mouth slanted roughly over hers as if he couldn't restrain himself any longer.

"Quinn," she groaned, dragging her lips from his. "You're hurting me."

He stopped instantly. His hand pulled her head to his chest while his fingers entwined with her hair, causing mass confusion in the carefully styled curls. Expelling his breath with a jagged sigh, he rested his head on top of hers. "I'm sorry, my love," he apologized. "I don't know what came over me. I was frustrated and took my anger out on you."

Meggie could feel the muscles working convulsively along his jaw and recognized the emotional turmoil he was struggling to contain. But why? What had he heard? What wasn't he telling her? The tight set of his mouth and jaw told Meggie he wasn't going to elaborate.

Instead of meeting her at the elevator the next morning, Quinn knocked on her door just as she'd finished dressing. Meggie answered his repeated rap, absently buckling the belt of her blue linen skirt.

"Good morning." He smiled and placed a brief kiss on her waiting lips.

"This is a surprise." She still hadn't slipped on her heels and yet they were almost at eye level with one another. "Be careful," she warned lovingly. "I could become very accustomed to a morning kiss."

"It's better than coffee," Quinn returned with a mocking glint in his eye. "Kissing you wakes me up more than I care to admit, but then sleeping with only a wall separating us isn't exactly inducing a peaceful night's rest." With one look at the glazed quality of her eyes, he laughed and placed a finger over her lips. "Don't say it."

Meggie hated to admit how close she had come

to fervently whispering his name and the guilty look that flashed across her face caused him to chuckle all the more.

"Can I take you to lunch again today?" he offered.

Retrieving her shoes from the bedroom, she used one hand to place the shoe on her foot and one hand on his arm to balance herself. "I don't know if I can take such stimulating conversation two days in a row."

"Meggie," his voice warned, but the corner of his mouth was quivering with suppressed amusement.

Their eyes met briefly. "All right, but Quinn," she took a deep breath, "you can't be with me every second."

"Yes, but not for lack of trying," he teased.

"Oh, honestly!" Meggie laughed.

He caught her off guard; wrapping his arms around her he claimed her mouth in a long, sensuous kiss that sent her world careening.

"What was that for?" she questioned breathlessly, her hand tracing the outline of his kiss over her throbbing mouth.

The effect of the exchange was obviously more than he'd bargained for, as he responded with a forced effort. "I just wanted to congratulate you for not saying 'Oh, Quinn.' "

Hands linking them together, they headed for the elevator.

· · ·

Meggie was busy finishing up the policies on her desk Friday afternoon.

"This relationship with the inspector must be getting serious," Carol commented at quitting time.

Meggie hadn't mentioned their unofficial engagement. She didn't feel comfortable telling others, not yet. At least not until she'd received an engagement ring.

"What makes you say that?" Meggie asked without looking up from her desk.

"Because he came to have lunch with you just a few hours ago and he's here again," she said with a wry twist to her mouth.

Meggie's head snapped up. "What?" For a moment she was sure her friend was teasing. But one look at the virile man walking across the polished floor confirmed Carol's words.

Leaning indolently against her desk, the palms of his hands supporting his weight, Quinn gazed down at her.

"What are you doing here?" she whispered furiously.

"What does it look like?" he answered, unaffected by her obvious lack of a welcome.

"Quinn," she murmured, conscious of the stares of her fellow workers. "This is getting to be ridiculous." She stood, taking her purse from the bottom desk drawer. "Besides, this constant attention is embarrassing me."

"Meggie, I love you," he said in a lowered voice as if that would appease her.

She flashed him a silencing look. "Quinn Donnelley, that simply isn't going to work."

"Maybe this will." He pulled out an oblong envelope from the inside pocket of his suit coat and handed it to her.

Meggie sat back down as she accepted the piece of paper. "What's this?" Her voice was quiet, questioning.

"Open and see."

Confusion clouded the clarity of her dark eyes as she tore open the envelope. She glanced up hesitantly. "It's an airplane ticket. Where? Why?"

His hand at her elbow lifted her gently from the chair. "Come on, we'll talk about it on our way to the car."

Obediently, Meggie followed, too stunned to question him. She'd been so surprised she hadn't noticed the ticket's destination. The hand at her elbow was gripping her so tightly that she was sure there would be a bruise later.

Urgency filled his steps as he escorted her from the building. Instead of heading for the employee parking lot in the back of the building, Quinn brought her around to the customer parking lot, where his Jeep was waiting.

"What about my car?" she asked, pointing lamely in the other direction.

"George has promised to keep his eye on it until

you return. If it's more than a few days, I'll have it brought to the apartment, so don't worry about it."

"A few days?" Meggie pulled her arm free. "Just what's going on here?"

Quinn paused, thrusting long, tapered fingers through his hair. For the first time that day Meggie noticed the small lines of doubt and worry that were tightly etched about his eyes and mouth as if something monumentally heavy was weighing on him.

A prickling of fear raced over her skin, raising tiny goose bumps on her forearms. "Quinn, what is it? What did he say last night?" She didn't need to qualify whom she meant by "he." Quinn knew.

"You don't need to worry about it, Meggie; the whole thing's been arranged. But I'll feel a lot better if I know you're safe. Your father and I had a long talk this afternoon and he agreed the best place for you right now is home."

"Home," she repeated stiffly, "is right here in Portland with you and Jill."

His soft chuckle caught her unaware. "That's exactly what your father said you'd say." He hesitated. "Meggie, I want you to do this for me."

Stubbornly she shifted her weight from one foot to the other and crossed her arms in front of her. Ignoring the questioning, vaguely pleading look in his eye she asked, "How did you know dad's phone number?"

He shrugged. "From the phone bill on your bedroom dresser."

"And just when were you in my bedroom?" she demanded.

Quinn opened the door of the Jeep and Meggie saw one of her suitcases sitting in the back. "When I packed your bags," he responded, as if it were the most normal thing in the world for him to go into her apartment and sort through her things. The sudden thought of him searching through her drawers brought a flood of color to her face.

"Did you get everything?" she asked, her voice slightly flustered. The way some women collect hats or shoes, Meggie collected lacy underthings. "Don't you need a warrant or something?"

"I'm looking forward to seeing you in some of that fancy gear," he whispered just loud enough for her to hear, causing her to blush all the more.

"Quinn Donnelley, you are no gentleman," she replied stiffly, knocking the hand he offered her aside. He was still chuckling to himself as he walked around the other side of the car. The fiery glance she threw him as she sat erect quickly quelled his amusement.

Inserting the car key into the ignition, Quinn cleared his throat. Silently, they rode together to the airport. When he stopped for a red light several miles from Hadley Insurance, his hand left the steering wheel. Without a word he placed it on top of hers, which lay on the seat. The action dissolved Meggie's indignation. It wasn't that he had gone into her apartment and packed her things. But he was forcing her to do something she'd never wanted to do again: run from a problem. In her own mind she realized she wasn't. It was Quinn who needed the assurance that she was safe while he dealt with whoever was making the calls. He hadn't told her what he was going to do, what action he had planned. She wasn't sure she wanted to know.

"I won't stay any longer than the weekend," she informed him in a proper voice that she hoped conveyed the strength of her will.

His returning smile related his own determination. "We'll see," he said.

"Yes, we will," she said forcefully.

Quinn's hand returned and tightened around the steering wheel. For a moment Meggie thought he was angry until she realized that he was having difficulty restraining his laughter. "I didn't realize you were one of those females who had to have the last word."

"I'm not," she defended herself with a righteous glare.

"I'm glad to hear it."

"Good." She remained stiff and erect, her gaze focused directly ahead of her. She chose to ignore his soft chuckle. Turning her head she studied the shops and businesses along the route, her mouth pressed tightly shut. If he'd said one more thing she would have disgraced herself by bursting into tears. Visiting her dad wasn't the way to solve the problem. She didn't want to fly home. Her life was here in Portland and she was proud of all that she had accomplished in these short months. When she'd first arrived she didn't know a soul. Now she had a home, a man she loved with her heart and soul, good friends . . . and one sickie. Of its own volition her bottom lip began to quiver as the first tears filled her eyes. Why would anyone want to do this to her? It was beginning to turn her whole life upside down. Again she'd miss seeing Jill over the weekend. The need to talk to the girl forced an involuntary sob deep from within Meggie's throat. She bit into her trembling lip, praying Quinn hadn't noticed.

"Meggie?" A questioning note filled his voice.

Hurriedly she wiped the tears from her face before turning to look at him and smiling brightly. "Yes?" she replied with feigned cheerfulness.

His eyes studied her, narrowing as he noted the damp eyelashes and the proud tilt of her chin. "You're not fooling me," he said, momentarily returning his attention to the street.

Meggie gave him a brave smile. He was using the same words she'd spoken the other day when she had informed him she knew exactly what he was doing by taking her to lunch. "I know," she whispered softly, lowering her gaze to the neatly folded hands that rested in her lap.

After parking the Jeep and checking in her suitcase, Quinn said, "Your father will pick you up at the airport."

Meggie answered with an abrupt nod.

His hand gripped hers as they walked silently down the concourse. They sat next to one another until her flight was called for boarding. Somehow, deep inside, Meggie had the inescapable sensation this was all some horrible nightmare and that she'd wake in an hour or two and find the whole thing had been a bad dream. Closing her eyes, she inhaled deeply, praying the dream would end.

"Meggie," Quinn said softly, his hand linked to hers pulling her upright. "I don't want you to go. But I'm asking you to trust me in this." With infinite care his hand cupped her face as he gently laid his mouth over hers for the sweetest, most beautiful kiss Meggie had ever received.

Drowning in the depth of her love, Meggie slumped against him, tears filling her eyes. It was impossible to speak; the knot in her throat had grown so large it was difficult to breathe. It was as if someone had cut off her oxygen supply.

Halfway into the Jetway, Meggie turned around to look back. People boarding the plane stepped around her. "Did you forget something, miss?" a stewardess asked.

Meggie shook her head, weaving her way between the others. As soon as she was out of the Jetway she saw Quinn. He was standing at the window looking at her plane, his gaze following the progress of the boarding passengers as the window seats were taken. He seemed to be waiting for her to look out from the plane window and wave. He stood with his back twisted away from her until she softly called his name.

For an instant he looked shocked to see her. Their eyes locked in a duel of wills. With a delicate movement of her lips she smiled, conceding. She raised her hand to her mouth, kissed her fingers and with the same hand waved good-bye. Without another word, she turned and boarded the aircraft.

"Meggie." Roy O'Halloran stepped away from the crowd of people, his hand raised as he signaled to gain her attention.

"Dad." As much as she hadn't wanted to leave Portland and Quinn, Meggie couldn't prevent the flood of pleasure she felt at seeing her father again. She returned his wave eagerly and hurried through the throng of passengers that were impeding her progress.

They hugged one another as if it'd been years instead of a few months since they'd bidden their farewells.

"Meggie, let me look at you." Her father broke

the contact and gleamed a golden smile at her. "Love seems to agree with you."

Involuntarily, Meggie blushed as she tucked a strand of hair around her ear.

"Quinn sounds like the kind of son-in-law I'd hoped you'd pick. You've chosen well."

Meggie couldn't restrain the smile that curved up the corners of her soft mouth. For so long her father had only seen Sam as a suitable husband, and to have him say otherwise amazed her.

"And just who said anything about Quinn and me getting married?" she questioned indignantly. Although Meggie mentioned Quinn and Jill in nearly every telephone conversation with her father, she had never said anything about their decision to marry.

"Oh dear," Roy groaned, "I didn't let the cat out of the bag, did I? Quinn asked me if I had any objections to the two of you. While you're home he wanted the two of us to select a day for the wedding. I just naturally assumed . . ." He let the rest of what he was going to say fade away.

Looping her hand in his elbow, Meggie smiled with an inner happiness. "Honestly, Dad, of course he's asked me. It just surprised me that he said anything to you, that's all. And, Dad, you're going to love Jill. She'll remind you so much of me at thirteen. How do you feel about being a grandfather?"

"Funny thing, Quinn not mentioning his

daughter." Her father ran a hand over his unshaven cheek. "I kept expecting him to say something about Jill and a ready-made family. Of course, I knew about the girl from everything you've said. But Quinn didn't mention her once. Not a word."

The bubble of happiness that surrounded Meggie seemed to burst all at once. Jill was nothing more than an encumbrance in Quinn's life. An ache grew in Meggie's heart for the child Quinn found impossible to love.

Sam was waiting for them when they arrived home from the airport. Meggie walked into the small home and felt the comfort of familiar things, a deep sense of belonging. Sam was sitting on the worn sofa, leafing through a dog-eared magazine. He laid it aside the minute Meggie walked in the door.

Roy walked around his daughter, carrying her suitcase into her bedroom.

"Hello, Sam," she said, and smiled softly.

Hesitatingly he stood, his eyes focusing on the pattern of the old carpet. "Welcome home," he murmured in a dejected, hurt tone. "I've missed you, Meggie."

"What a nice thing to say. It's good to be home for a visit." She qualified her arrival, making sure he understood she would only be there a few days.

Sam nodded. "Roy said you're going to marry some hot-shot policeman in Portland."

Holding her purse with both hands in front of her skirt, Meggie said, "Quinn's an inspector for the Portland police."

For the briefest second Meggie saw something unreadable flicker over Sam's face. "I wish you every happiness, Meggie."

"Thank you, Sam, I know you mean that." It was an uncomfortable scene; she didn't know what more she could say and, for lack of words, stood on the far side of the room just inside the front door.

"I don't know about you, Meggie," her father interrupted the silence from the kitchen doorway, "but I could do with a cup of cocoa."

Meggie smiled at her father gratefully. "Me, too," she agreed in an eager voice, happy to be on familiar ground. "Want one, Sam?"

He shook his head, his eyes still managing to avoid hers. "I've got to be heading home. It was nice seeing you again, Meggie."

"You too, Sam," she finished with a breathy sigh.

"Meggie," Sam stopped, his hand on the doorknob. "Do you think your inspector friend would mind if I took you out to dinner Sunday afternoon? It would just be for old times' sake."

Meggie hesitated. There had been plenty of such dinners with Sam; she knew this one would be a repeat of all the others. First he'd tell her how much he loved her, had always loved her, how his life would be incomplete without her. The experience was enough to take away a starving man's appetite.

"I'm leaving Sunday. I don't know that we'd have time."

"Quinn didn't say anything about you flying out Sunday," her father interrupted.

Meggie flashed him a fiery glare. "Nonetheless, I'm returning to Portland Sunday afternoon."

Roy O'Halloran chuckled as he took the milk from the refrigerator.

"I could take you to the airport, Meggie," Sam offered. "I'll pick you up early in the afternoon; we could have brunch and then I could drive you to the airport."

Meggie wasn't sure she should agree. But if Quinn had told her father about the reason for her unexpected visit, it wouldn't be beyond him to make excuses to detain her. It would be just like Quinn to have set up such an arrangement.

"All right, Sam," she said. "That sounds like a good idea."

Her father hesitated, opening and closing his mouth as if he had something he wanted to say. Apparently he decided it wasn't worth saying because he resumed his task, taking a pan from the cupboard.

Quinn called Meggie Saturday afternoon, but she was shopping with a former school friend and missed the call. When she tried to return his call later, there was no answer.

Another call came for her early Sunday morning immediately after she'd left for Sunday school and church. Again her father said he thought it must have been Quinn. She was scheduled to fly out that afternoon and didn't attempt to return his call. After all, she'd be seeing him in a few hours anyway.

Her suitcase was packed for the return flight and she was waiting for Sam when the doorbell rang. Her father was reading the Sunday paper.

"I'll get it, Dad, it's probably Sam." She glanced at her wrist watch and noted that for once in his life Sam was early.

The sight at the front door brought a startled gasp from Meggie. "Quinn," she choked on his name. His appearance, far more than his presence, shocked her. His hair, normally groomed and neat, was a rumpled mess. A dark stubble grew along the lines of his jaw and cheek as if he hadn't shaved since she'd departed Friday afternoon. His clothes looked as if he'd slept in them.

"Oh, Meggie." His voice cracked when he spoke.

Before she could even stop to catch her breath she was heaved into his arms and squeezed until the very oxygen was sucked from her lungs.

"Quinn," she said in a tiny voice. "What is it?"

He eased her away from him and looked at her with such an infinite tenderness it brought a frown of inquisitiveness to Meggie's face. As if suddenly realizing where he was, Quinn pulled his gaze away from Meggie and flickered to her father, who was standing, looking just as shocked as Meggie.

"Quinn." Roy O'Halloran extended his hand.

Pulling Meggie into the crook of one arm, he shook hands with his future father-in-law with the other hand. "I'm sorry to meet you under these circumstances, Roy."

"Circumstances, what circumstances?" Meggie questioned.

"I've had a warrant issued for Sam Abernathy this morning. The L.A. police are picking him up now."

"Sam!" Both Meggie and her father cried simultaneously. Roy lowered himself onto the couch as if he couldn't believe what he was hearing.

"I'm sorry to be the one to bring such bad news," Quinn said in an apologetic tone. "But it was Sam who was making all the calls."

Meggie joined her father on the couch, her knees suddenly so shaky she felt unsteady. "But how, why?" Disbelief clouded reason. Of course Sam had motive to want to frighten her, scare her into returning to California. But she would never have suspected him of making long distance obscene calls.

Roy O'Halloran slumped forward, his knees supporting his elbows as he buried his face in his hands. "I should have realized . . . I should have known. Sam was always so confident Meggie would move back. But I'd never have believed he'd resort to this."

Kneeling beside her on the carpet, Quinn took her hands in his. "Thank God, you're safe," he murmured over and over, until he'd composed himself enough to explain what had happened. "You've talked so little about Sam, I didn't really make the connection until there were no calls Friday night. Saturday I started to suspect something was up and ordered a record of long-distance calls made to your number. One telephone number had made repeated calls. When I checked out the number I learned it was Sam's."

Several hours later Meggie sat beside Quinn on the airplane flying north. His hand continued to tightly grip hers, as if he couldn't let her out of his sight.

"I thought I'd lost you, Meggie," he murmured, in a deep guttural tone that spoke of untold anxiety. "I phoned your father this morning to try and warn him what was happening. But the line was a poor one and all I could get out of him was the fact you were flying home today and that Sam was taking you to the airport. I've never known such fear as when I heard him tell me you were meeting Sam. Before I could say or do anything your father said it was useless to try and talk on such a bad line and hung up the phone. When I tried to call back there wasn't an answer."

"Dad works in the garage on Sunday mornings. He just didn't hear the phone, that's all," she explained.

Covering her hand with both of his, he looked away for a moment. "Do you remember me saying I didn't pray? I told you there wasn't anything important enough in my life to pray about. But I prayed today as I've never done before." He rubbed a hand over his face and for a moment Meggie was sure she saw a sheen of tears glimmer in the depth of his eyes. "You were right when you said I've been tortured by guilt. Diana, Nelson, Laura—I've never laid them to rest. I've blamed myself for what happened; I allowed hate and bitterness to discolor my life." He swallowed tightly and Meggie squeezed his hand, bringing the callused fingers to her mouth as if she could kiss away the hurt. "You were right about Jill, too," he said in a soft tone. "Of all, she is innocent in this. I've decided from now on Jill is my daughter. I'll probably never know the truth, but it doesn't matter. I've made her my daughter in my heart."

"Oh, Quinn," Meggie said, and tried to hold back the tears. For the first time that afternoon, Quinn smiled, his eyes gazing deeply into hers. "I was like a crazy man trying to get to you. When I couldn't connect with a commercial flight, I hired a private plane. You aren't going to believe this but the pilot was a retired clergyman."

A gentle smile touched her face, reaching her eyes so that they glinted with all the love that burned in her heart. "Of course I believe it. My God works in mysterious ways."

Quinn's eyes locked with hers. "Our God, Meggie," he corrected. "I've done a lot of things in my life that I regret, but today I am a new man, free in Christ. The past is buried and the future—our future—holds wonderful promises."

Meggie laid her head on his shoulder and closed her eyes, her heart overflowing with a happiness that made words impossible.

"Meggie, come look," Jill insisted. She was wearing faded jeans and a T-shirt her new grandfather had printed for her. The picture on the front was of a Cheshire cat grinning his know-it-all smile but his teeth were wired with braces. "I've got my room unpacked," she told Meggie proudly. "It really looks great."

Meggie stood in the open doorway, her hair contained in a bright kerchief while boxes from the moving van littered the house. "Jill, this is great. Good enough for you to help me arrange the living room."

Jill laughed, her young face sparkling with

happiness. "You know adults are really funny sometimes?"

Meggie paused, hands on her hips. "Oh, and how's that?"

Jill placed one of the moving boxes into her closet. "Right before you and Dad got married, I think it was while you were in California. Anyway Dad came to talk to Hariette and when he saw me he murmured something about the braces and started hugging me like crazy. That's when Dad and I had our talk. Then when you saw me you took one look at me, covered your mouth with your hand and started laughing and crying and hugging me just like Dad had done." She paused, her eyes meeting Meggie's across the width of the room. "I think adults can act crazy sometimes."

Meggie didn't even try to make excuses, only smiled softly to herself.

"Meggie, Jill, I'm back," Quinn called from the front door. "I hope everyone likes cheeseburgers for our first dinner in our new home." Long strides ate up the distance between them as he handed Jill the sack and pulled Meggie into his arms. "Come here, woman, we forgot something."

"Quinn," she cried, as he pulled her out the front door and ceremoniously lifted her into his arms. Automatically, she looped her arms around his neck. "You're crazy, you know that."

He chuckled. "Crazy in love," he murmured beside her ear.

"Just what are you doing?" Meggie demanded, unable to restrain the laughter.

"Atoning for an oversight. I wanted to carry you over the threshold this afternoon when the movers left, but we got so busy I forgot."

Jill stood in the entryway looking out after them, the sound of her giggles filling the summer's evening air. "See what I mean, Meggie?" she called. "Adults act sillier than kids sometimes."

Meggie looked dreamily into her husband's eyes. "Yes, they do," she admitted in a husky whisper. "They really do."

Center Point Large Print
600 Brooks Road / PO Box 1
Thorndike ME 04986-0001 USA

(207) 568-3717

US & Canada:
1 800 929-9108
www.centerpointlargeprint.com